THE CONIUM REVIEW

vol. 6

Conium Press
Portland, OR

The Conium Review
Vol. 6
© 2017 Conium Press
Portland, OR

http://www.coniumreview.com

ISBN-10 1-942387-13-X
ISBN-13 978-1-942387-13-8
ISSN 2164-6252

Cover Image: © dmitriy_kras / Adobe Stock
Internal Images: © dule964 / Adobe Stock
Layout & Design: James R. Gapinski

THE CONIUM REVIEW
vol. 6

James R. Gapinski
Managing Editor

Chelsea Werner-Jatzke
Outreach Coordinator

Holly Lopez
Associate Editor

Stephen Graham Jones
Contest Judge

Marina Petrova
Fiction Editor

William VanDenBerg
Fiction Editor

[contents]

[contents]

RAMUNE

Tamara K. Walker

RAMUNE

Tamara K. Walker

Get me some ramune, the chalkboard says. *I'm horribly antiquated. Ramune is hip. It's what everyone's drinking these days. It's the next happening thing.*

I don't know where or why you got that impression, I respond, silently as usual. *Yes, it's popular, but not everyone drinks it. And it's been around for a while. It's not a new trend.*

Look, you think it's easy? It isn't. I'm surprised that I'm not construction scrap by this point. I'm archaic, and I deserve ramune. Whiteboards drink it. And those newfangled touchscreen projector boards, I'm sure they have it. Red strawberry ramune for them. Go. Get. Some.

!

The chalkboard becomes so agitated that a single bold exclamation point appears in green dust, breaking our pact. I quickly erase it with my thumb.

"Well, I think you're being quixotic about yourself, but if you'd like, I'll try to fetch some ramune." I act as if I'm picking up my phone, so no one knows we're talking aloud like this. "Please remember the pact."

I begin researching places to find ramune on my new tablet. Several nearby convenience stores turn up on a map, the closest only a quarter of a mile away. I point.

The chalkboard hesitates.

—I remain skeptical, but if they have ramune, that'll be fine. My desire for it is quite extreme.

. . .

Taking a bicycle, I arrive in a few minutes. I search everywhere for the beverage: high and low, up and down, in and out. It's nowhere to be found. I approach the cashier, a stoic, gray, bipedal ram with bulbous horns.

"Ra-mu-ne?" I mouth the shrugging syllables.

"We don't have it," he replies. I notice some brand-new bottles behind his head, however, full of bright fizzy liquid and topped with marbles.

"But—right there!" I timidly gesture to the ramune, which I'm quite certain now is in fact ramune, the katakana characters on the labels visible as I squint.

"We don't," he says more emphatically, in a polite tone that threatens anger if I fail to accept this.

"Is it possible you've forgotten? I see the bottles behind you, right there."

The cashier is getting bored. "Those are empty bottles for recycling."

"No, they're full of liquid," I persist. *I just want some damn ramune to satisfy my chalkboard lover*, I want to scream. But of course I can't. The pact. "If they're empty recycling, then why are they on display?"

The cashier looks irritated by my question, which seems in his mind to be moot. He leans his head back and groans, softly tapping the shelving with his horns. "—I don't know. That's just where we keep them, I guess to encourage people to recycle. Look, they're empty. We're out of ramune right now. See for yourself." He laconically takes a bottle from the shelf and sets it down on the counter in front of me. I pick it up to slosh the translucent soda around, partly to verify its existence and partly to brag.

After the third or fourth rotation in my hand, the bottle feels much lighter and the sloshing stops. I glance down and see that the cashier was telling the truth. It's empty.

"Ah." I swallow, feeling dizzy. "I'm sorry to have bothered you." He gives me a smug, irked look. I regain my speech faculties for a moment. "When are you expecting new stock?"

"Yesterday." He starts straightening things up behind the counter, his hooves clicking everywhere on hard surfaces.

"Aha, so it's late then?"

He shoots me a befuddled expression. "No."

"Uh—" I'm not quite sure how to respond. "You said you were expecting it yesterday, and it isn't here…"

"Yes. We are expecting it yesterday, and of course it isn't here yet." I'm extraneous. He's fully going about his business, having evidently written me off.

"Um—well—ok—when's the soonest you expect it'll get here? Tomorrow?"

"Best-case scenario? The day before the day before yesterday." He turns his back to me and walks off to a storage room.

I sputter at his absence but no words come. Pivoting quickly on my heels, I hastily exit the store.

■　　■　　■

The chalkboard is displeased. *They didn't have it?* Now a look of self-pity and concern. I'm worried.

"Afraid not. I'll check other stores tomorrow." We seem to be in private, so I chance verbal speech. "Can't we just—" I stroke the border sensually with my fingertips, micro-massaging the crevices between writing surface and metal. I lean in exaggeratedly and breathily sigh in a desperate parody of seduction, but the chalkboard's stiff, fretful manner is unyielding.

The chalkboard sighs. *I know I said before that I wanted ramune because I'm insecure about my obsolescence, but the truth is—*

I understand, I interject. No one's around but this is more intimate. Our special communication. *You're not outdated to me.* I pat the chalk tray reassuringly.

—the truth is, I'm awfully thirsty. I didn't want to tell you this before because I didn't want you to worry, but I'm dehydrated and the situation is actually rather dire. All this chalk is drying me out. People feed me chalk, day after day, and I haven't the tiniest drop to wash it down with. I need ramune very soon.

"Ok," I blurt out, startled by this revelation. "Do you want me to check the other convenience stores?"

No. Thank you for checking but it won't be there. I've been thinking, and in consideration of things it isn't all that surprising that the convenience store didn't have it. No, I think the best place to find ramune is where you have unresolved memories.

Unresolved memories? I require further clarification, but the chalkboard is silent. Uncomfortable quiet fills the room like a bubble of methane released from melting permafrost.

.   .   .

I'm in my elementary school cafeteria. It's dark.

I have memories here of a snobbish yet generous second-grade classmate sharing ramune with me during lunchtime an eighth of an eternity ago. My first taste of the stuff. I recall being nonplussed at the taste, actually, but she showed me how to open it and the shape of the bottle made it that much more interesting. I promised to reciprocate with something tasty from my lunch, but I was never able. Uncertain about approaching her, as we didn't have an established friendship, I dithered for the rest of the year and then she moved. Despite her icy personality, the disparity in our social status, and the suddenness of the gesture, I didn't perceive her offer of ramune as condescension at all.

I hope this memory qualifies. The chalkboard didn't say that the memories had to be unresolved memories of ramune itself.

The cafeteria is full of adults. Nameless, faceless, ageless people all blend into each other, sometimes sidestepping close and conjoining cloth and flesh where they convert into gray slime at the point of contact before melding. I wonder what would happen if they got stuck there, in that gray gunk quasi-fused state with two unmelted, unmatched halves. They lack nametags, which is why they're nameless, they lack pictures on those nametags, which is why they're faceless, and the only indication of age is that I know some of them are in college. The only person I recognize is a semi-popular local musician, who sits cross-legged at one of the long tables and watches the room with bereaved amusement.

"You here for the conference?" a man with a chartreuse messenger bag shaped like a bottle of moisturizer brusquely inquires. His head glows florescent white faintly. Before I can answer, he wedges past me and I notice the wiry frayed antennae emerging from his cervical vertebrae. They look like they've seen better days.

"That's ok, neither am I, neither is anyone here," he mutters.

When the antenna-moisturizer-bag man passes, I can make out the glow behind his head. It's across the cafeteria, in the corner adjacent to the kitchen and the exit doors leading out to the playground. A vending machine, converted into a simple beverage fridge. No credits needed. Through the glass, I see rows of ramune bottles. Reaching in, I remember that the chalkboard didn't specify a preferred flavor. I grab one arbitrarily and head down the hallway toward the classrooms, the din of the cafeteria people echoing in my head.

Halfway to my second-grade classroom, I realize that the bottle in my hand lacks a plastic cap with the plunger necessary to open it. I head back, retracing my steps, and find that the cafeteria is as noisy as ever, flooded with the sounds of chattering and walking and melding, but vacant. Slippery gray people-melding gunk coats the linoleum floor. The beverage fridge is now a rather expensive vending machine. My pockets are as empty as the cafeteria. I yawn and sprint to the classroom.

■   ■   ■

Aa, Bb, Cc, Dd, Ee— the poster on the ceiling reads, cursive example letters printed waveringly across squiggly lines. The chalkboard, my chalkboard, is there. I hold the ramune bottle up to the light triumphantly and gelatin color reflects onto the chalkboard's parched face.

I don't have a plunger to sink the marble, I say. *I'll just use something else to open it. I'll pry it open with a screwdriver.*

The chalkboard hesitates, and I sense that something's seriously wrong. *What is it?*

Psssssh. The chalkboard takes a deep breath and exhales in a thin stream. *That won't work. I—I need to do this. Oh, this is embarrassing.*

I'll just open it. Here, here's a screwdriver in the desk.

I'm not really all that thirsty, the chalkboard admits. *That was just a cover-up, too. I'm humiliated, but you deserve the truth, my devoted paramour. The truth of the matter—the real truth, not the shell-truth I told you to obscure its soft fleshy body—is that I'm troubled about my agency. I can't do anything by myself. Everyone with arms and hands and legs has to do everything for me. It's beyond exasperating.*

I try to soothe my love with a gentle touch and a sympathetic mien, though I can feel my spirits start to roil. *Even if we had a plunger, how do you intend to open a ramune bottle with no help?*

Hold the plunger flat against me and push. Relatively speaking, I'd be moving to open it and you'd be standing still. I know I'd need a little help to get things going, but it's better than nothing. It's better than now.

I peek at the bottle again, and— voilà—we indeed have a plastic plunger, just as it's supposed to be capped over the marble. It punches itself out of the cap and zips around the room, pinballing off the walls. Finally closing my hands around it as it settles down, I feel that it has become chalk again. I align it against the marble and intimate offering it to the chalkboard's cheek.

No, no, NO! the chalkboard stresses uncharacteristically. *I'm desperately dehydrated. I can't bear the slightest bit more of chalk.*

You just said that it was about agency.

Yes, I did.

The only plunger we have now is a chalk one.

That is a dilemma, the chalkboard opines as I slam my palm desperately downward and the chalk plunger crumbles to dust on the shimmering marble.

HOLY WATER

Jay Vera Summer

HOLY WATER

Jay Vera Summer

I am standing in the cafeteria of Larkin High School in Elgin, Illinois, and I want to have sex. I haven't seen this room in over a decade, but it looks the same: white cinderblock walls, rows of long, brown folding tables with round seats attached. This is the first time I've seen it empty of people. Water drips down the walls and pools at least a foot deep, seeping into my gym shoes. I remember seeing a guy light a girl's hair on fire in this room when I was a student. Too bad the water wasn't here then.

A man sloshes from around the corner about fifty feet away and walks until he's right in front of me. He's an older version of the guy who lit the girl's hair on fire, and he's more attractive. He's in jeans and a gray t-shirt. Maybe it's the same guy, and he grew hotter over time, or maybe it's the guy's brother. I always feel bad when I meet brothers who look almost identical except somehow one is hot and one is not, like they are the attractive and ugly versions of the same man. I feel bad now. He stares at me, but I don't know what he is. I think I'd have sex with him.

"Are you a ghost?" I ask.

"No." He shakes his wet, brown hair out of his brown

eyes, which then stare at me.

"Touch my arm," he says. "If I am a ghost, your hand will go right through me."

I touch his arm, and it feels great. I want to stroke it, to kiss it. But maybe it is too good to be real, exactly how a trick ghost arm would probably feel to the sex-starved living.

"Hold on," I say, pulling my iPhone out of my jean shorts' back pocket. I navigate to the App Store, type in "ghost detector," then download the first free app that comes up. "I'm not connected to Wi-Fi right now so this could take a minute."

I look at the app, wishing it would hurry. I look at him. Those eyes. That hair. It's dry now, and curly. It's growing a little, puffing up.

He holds out his hand, and I grab it. We are eye-to-eye. My fingers tingle; then the feeling travels up my forearm to my shoulder, down to my stomach, and finally my vagina. I look at his hand, wondering how it could have such a powerful effect on me. It's both soft and strong with short, clean nails. I think about unzipping my jean shorts and leading his hand into my underwear, which is white cotton. Putting his hand where I want it without breaking eye contact. Sitting on the floor, right here in high school, and having him finger me under the water. I imagine myself rocking back so my hair gets wet and him pulling me forward from the inside.

"Jessica," he says.

Something is wrong. I grab his hand and try to remember. I feel a chill and throw his hand away.

"My name! I never told you my name." I'm shaking.

He smiles, and his teeth are white, but he's shrinking, fading. Small waves lap at my calves. My phone beeps, and I look down. The ghost detector is downloaded and going nuts with warning bells. A big red dot pulsates just above center in the green and black radar screen.

He reaches for me and mouths my name, but I don't hear anything except for the ghost detector beeps. I raise my arm to slap him, but my hand travels through him and he dissipates into droplets that fall to the floor. I stumble and trip into the water face first.

I stretch open my eyes. The water is blue and clear and doesn't sting. I see a large orange goldfish swimming, an abandoned shoe. I bob my head above the surface and feel the floor below me fall, so the water is too deep for me to touch the bottom. I look around, and find I'm in Chicago on Milwaukee Avenue, treading at the Western stoplight turned red. The sun is bright.

The tops of parallel-parked cars peek out from under slow-moving waves. The sidewalks are flooded, but just a foot or so because concrete is visible through the water. The street, however, is bottomless. Two gators swim up next to me on the left. They make faces that might be attempts at smiles. They are blue, my favorite color.

"Why are you here?" I ask.

"We followed you from Florida," they say in unison, laughing. Their teeth are sharp and yellow. I remember I live in Florida. I hope I haven't been gone too long, haven't lost my job.

"When and why did I leave?"

"Just today, for the same reason we followed you." They laugh.

"And why are you blue?"

"Illinois is a blue state. We try to be respectful, fit in."

The stoplight turns green and the gators pass me. I see concrete steps ahead on the right that lead to nowhere. I swim over and hoist myself up. Maybe the steps once led to playground equipment, or a happy home. Sitting, I put my head in my hands. When I look up, there is a man in a tuxedo sitting next to me. He has black and silver hair and ice blue eyes. His hair is styled perfectly—I can see grooves where the comb last passed through it.

"Are you a terrorist?" I ask. At my age, there's no point in beating around the bush.

"What's that supposed to mean?" he says. He smiles, and his teeth look like chalk.

"I just dealt with someone who wasn't what he seemed, so I figure I'd ask."

"You got me! I don't usually mention it, but I'm a social terrorist, on weekends mostly. I have a day job but feel more called to terrorism. It's how I express myself. The day job is for money. A guy's gotta eat."

"Do you eat pussy?" I ask. I want to shock him and gauge his reaction. Maybe it'll help me figure out if we should have sex.

"No, I terrorize it. Sorry. Try to keep those two worlds separate. You understand."

"Yeah." I pull out my phone. The ghost detector is open, but silent.

"But you really knew I was a terrorist, right away? That's great. Usually only Muslim social terrorists get called out, and c'mon, that's just racism, let's be real."

"Okay," I say, "let's be real. Tell me something real right now."

"Real? Well," he leans in and grabs my shoulders, "you gave me the biggest compliment anyone has ever given me. You viewed me how I view myself. No, how I *want* to be viewed. Actually, no, you viewed me as the person I aspire to be rather than the person I am now. That's life-affirming. People pay millions for that, you know? And you just gave it away. And here's the thing—it is worth so much more to me because you gave it away."

"I think I read a study about that," I say, glad he finally stopped talking. "Oh wait, no, it was the opposite. People value things more when they pay for them."

"It boils down to trust. When people get certain things for free, like a toothbrush from a stranger, they don't trust. 'Why is this free?' they wonder. 'Maybe something is wrong with it,' they think. But your compliment is no toothbrush—if I bought it, I'd trust it less. If I bought it, that'd indicate it wasn't genuine."

He stares at me and his eyes grow bluer. I can tell he's excited about what he said, that he wants me to be excited, too. "That's deep," I lie.

"Thank you." We sit and look at the water. My legs are tan. My gym shoes are white which makes my calves look even tanner. My shorts are acid wash, which makes me feel cool. I realize the man is still there and staring at me.

"So what's your favorite kind of terrorism?" I ask, not that terrorism is a particular interest of mine.

"I try to get creative. That's the benefit of not being a full-time terrorist. Artistic freedom."

"Do you ever think you'll terrorize full-time?"

"No. You get hired to terrorize and sooner or later they're going to want you to murder or martyr. I'm not that kind of terrorist—no death for me."

He stares at me. I try to remember what he wants. "I believe it. You're very convincing."

"Thanks. Death is very anti-terrorism. Terrorism is about fear and the dead aren't afraid. Plus, when you murder, that's one less person available to terrorize. And if you martyr, that's one less terrorist on the planet.

Hopefully I can start a paradigm shift. How long can terrorism as an art continue if all the best terrorists martyr themselves?"

"I believe you will go down in history as one of the best terrorists," I say, "And I want you to kiss me because of it."

He closes his eyes. I watch his gelled, black and silver hair shake as it gets closer, until my eyes cross. He kisses me. It feels like a giant worm wriggling into my face. I pull away.

"Why are you licking the inside of my mouth?" I ask.

"It's French kissing. Haven't you done that before?"

"I have. Sorry."

"You forgot? It must have been a long time."

"It felt different before. Not like licking, not like an animal in my mouth. The other times, it felt more like two parts of my own mouth moving around."

The tuxedoed man laughs and leans in again to kiss me. I hold my hand out. "I wish you well," I say, "but I must swim off. Please don't follow me."

He bites his lip, and I am briefly struck by his beauty until I remember his worm tongue. It's a shame when beautiful people are secretly revolting.

I stand and leap, belly-flopping onto the water. I swim down a side street and under an underpass. When I emerge from the other side, I'm on an empty football field that is only a few inches under water. I stand and walk across the field then climb onto the empty bleachers and sit alone. I look around and contemplate masturbating. I don't see anyone, but it's a big space. Suddenly, a man sits down next to me. He has blond hair and green eyes. He's wearing 1970s-style red and white piped track shorts and a tank top.

"Good thing I kept my clothes on," I say to him. I wouldn't be surprised if he's the star quarterback, to tell the truth. He looks fresh off a game or practice or maybe a beer party.

He leans in to kiss me and I pull away. "What's wrong?" he asks.

"I don't know," I say, looking down and biting my lip. I move my bottom lip back and forth between my teeth, stalling for time. "I guess I don't know what you are yet."

"Ha, ha, just a jock. And you don't have to know me much for kissing anyway." He runs his fingers through his hair and the sun glitters off it.

"I just need to make sure you're not my dad."

"I am so not your dad. I have a really good sense of humor." At this, he throws his head back and laughs and laughs. It echoes across the sky.

"So does he." I feel something in the back of my throat, maybe vomit.

"I'm also super smart, though."

"My dad is very intelligent."

"I bet he's not shy. I'm shy. Really shy. Like right now. I am so nervous around you I can't say a word. Look at me, I'm paralyzed."

"My dad is reserved," I say. "Much quieter than you are."

He leans in and pushes his tongue into my mouth. It feels like a scary snake at first, but then so does mine. They are two water moccasins skating across the top of a pool in unison.

I take my shirt off and look down. The sight of my breasts excites me. I take his shirt off and touch his chest hair. It's blond, just like the hair on his head. He ruins everything by saying, "Do you want to have sex with your dad?"

"No, that's the entire issue here. That's why I was making sure you aren't him."

"I've always wanted to have sex with my mom, kind of," he says.

"Oh. Um." I don't know if I should dive under the bleachers or offer to roleplay. There are tears in his eyes.

"She'd hate me if she knew." He buries his face in his hands and weeps.

"She wouldn't. She would forgive you. It's motherly instinct. It's science. I read a study."

"Really?" he asks, perking up. "In a credible academic journal or just online?"

"In an academic journal," I say. "Peer reviewed. Your mom wouldn't hate you."

"It's not about sex, really. I just don't want my mom to think her son's a loser."

"A loser?" I say. "With blond hair? About to have sex on hot metal bleachers in the sun?" At that, he gently pushes me onto my back, unzips my shorts, and pulls them down and off. I let my legs hang, one off each side of the bleacher. He starts having sex with me, and it is so good I close my eyes and moan. I open them to make sure this is real and notice a tattoo on his chest. It is three Greek symbols.

"You're in a fraternity?" I lay my head on the bleacher, limp, then puke off the side.

"Yeah," he says. He stops moving.

"Why'd you stop?" I ask.

"You're sick," he says.

"I thought that's how you'd like it."

He stares at me.

"Like, if you thought I was passed out."

He keeps staring.

"From alcohol, or roofies, I don't know. Because you're a frat boy."

"That's mean," he says.

"Are you still hard?"

He looks down. "Yes, but it doesn't mean I like you barfing during our lovemaking."

"Nerd!" I yell.

He stares at me. He looks sad.

"I won't throw up again," I say. "It was a joke."

"Fine," he says, then he puts himself back inside me. "I could do this forever."

I arch my back and smash my cheek into the silver bleacher, feeling its grooves press into my face. I start to finish, and he can tell. He rushes, trying to finish at the same time. It doesn't work, but I appreciate the effort. I cry a little from happiness but don't let him see. When he's done, he lays his head on my chest and his breathing is hard. Mine is almost non-existent, which feels unfair. I pet his hair and smell it. Sweat and fruit, or salt and sugar.

"I don't want you to think we're getting married," he says.

"Huh?"

"Because of what I said in the moment. The word 'forever.'"

"I'd never think that."

"Good, because I'm a commitment-phobe who only likes casual sex."

"You're not. If you were, you'd be doing this with a woman in a committed relationship, maybe, or one who lives somewhere impossible, across the country. You'd delude yourself into thinking you're open to real love but blocked from it by circumstance."

"Whoa," he says. "I used to be like that."

"And you probably didn't call yourself a commitment-phobe back then. Real commitment-phobes deny it. Recovering commitment-phobes admit it. When you say you're a commitment-phobe, you're really saying 'Don't hurt me.'" I trace circles in his chest hair. His chest is a field of corn.

"Wow," he says, "Maybe we *should* get married."

"I'm busy," I say. It's dumb, but it's the first thing that comes to my mind.

"If we don't get married, you'll forget about me, and then I'll be dead."

"Are you threatening to kill yourself?"

"Kill myself? I'm not separate from you. We're already together. I'll only die if you leave me."

I tap the bleacher hard and it hurts my finger. I pinch myself and that hurts too. I feel like I'm in a maze or untangling a necklace. He leans forward and kisses my breasts.

"So, if what you're saying is true, then you just want to use me," I say. "You don't want to marry me for love. You just don't want to die."

"If I didn't love you, why would I want to stay alive as part of you? I wouldn't."

"I don't know," I say. "Many people trudge through life miserably without explanation. It's not a simple matter of either love or death."

He lays his head on my chest again, and I kiss it and cry. If he really is part of me, I shouldn't feel bad letting him die. It'll be more like cutting my toenails or freezing off a wart than committing murder.

The sun has set. The sky grows darker, deeper, and

full of stars. They shine and twinkle, and I feel dazzled until I remember they're dead. They're all dead and have been dead for a long time. It just takes the human eye a while to register their light. Or is it that light itself takes a while to travel, regardless of the eye viewing it? This feels like an important distinction, but I can't quite figure it out. Tired of thinking, I close my eyes.

When I open my eyes, I hear cheers and feel warm. I feel pompons shaking against my cheeks and instinctually know that I am loved. I open my eyes. The blond guy is gone. I'm lying on the bleacher naked, in the sun, with a squad of cheerleaders in royal blue circled around me. They've been taking care of me, cheering me on.

"I don't even understand football," I say, tears in my eyes.

"We know," they coo in unison. "We're here to teach you everything."

They lean in, their long hair falling into my face. It smells like grapefruit. It's softer than my blankets at home and warmer. I want to fall asleep under it. I feel safe.

SOMETHING LIKE FEELING

Matthew Kirkpatrick

SOMETHING LIKE FEELING

Matthew Kirkpatrick

Cheryl and Tammers went to the art museum because of another fire at the mall. Tammers was worried at first but was relieved to hear that the Bon-Ton was spared. Cheryl hated the mall, and had told Tammers this, but Tammers never quite heard or didn't want to hear her because she loved everything about the mall—the smell of new clothing, the sound of the fountains, the taste of food court food. She loved the mall even when they weren't shopping, even when they were just sitting on a bench, splitting an Orange Julius, talking about all the great stuff at the mall.

"I love to watch all the people!" Tammers would say. "Doing things and going places!"

They'd had to pay for parking in a garage three blocks away, and the rain came down so hard their rain slickers had failed them as thick streams of water formed rivers in the creases of their jackets, directed onto their jeans and shoes. Their feet and legs were soaked, and here, in front of this painting, Cheryl contemplated the meaning of it all.

They'd started in the basement near the restrooms and coat check where the museum put the contemporary art.

Had they found a convenient parking space, and had it not been raining, she might have been more invested in what she saw: a naked man with no genitals, the height of a giant, surrounded by dismembered jaws, ears, and eyeballs. The figure of the man, like a doll, was scarred with wounds—precise, bloody slashes across his entire body.

Like Carl, she thought.

She knew the body and the eyeballs surrounding it were not real because the card next to the painting confirmed that though realistic, what was on display was still only a painting

I'm no idiot, she thought; *of course it's not real.* Was she supposed to *think* it was real? She hadn't seen another painting quite like this one, so had no model from which to judge it. Her instinct was that the painting was very bad, but here it was in the museum; what did she know?

The card told her the painting was a comment on gender. The wounded man had no genitals, so in a sense, his gender was muted both by the lack of a penis, the wounds on his body, the lack of clothing or other indicators. Desexualized. The body parts surrounding him, the card said, were the detritus of abject bodies, senses (taste, hearing, seeing) separate and discarded. Inputs without a central processor, according to the description.

"To what do they bear witness?" asked the card. Cheryl did not know. All she could fathom for herself was that the composition of the painting was symmetrical, and despite the unsettling image, she felt comfort in symmetry. She was more interested in the idea of a *real* wounded man, one who would pay somebody to mutilate him rather than ask his wife. She would have been happy to hit Carl, if he'd only told her that's what he'd wanted. She'd reluctantly agreed to a weekend trip to Florida in the coming weeks. She knew she would regret it, but he had been so insistent, promised it would be the last thing, really. They'd go and ride the dirty rides and watch the dirty shows, and he'd try to talk her into staying with him, and she would refuse. She'd probably have to refuse twice, maybe three times.

Cheryl took a photo of herself in front of the painting. Her face appeared in the photograph next to the man's sculpted torso and doll-crotch.

She followed Tammers, winding through a small crowd of others who, with their cameras and sticks, took photographs of themselves in front of the paintings, sculpture, and an installation replicating an office space.

They navigated the maze of soft blue cubicle walls, looking into each one of the roped off enclosures to gaze at the dusty desks and their contents: typewriters, old computers with CRT monitors, blurry photographs of families and pets. Effigies of workers slumped over their computer keyboards seemed to be the focus of the installation. Realistic pools of red-black blood from unseen head wounds oozed from the corpses across the surface of the desks.

The fake blood, like rich pudding, reminded Cheryl they'd have to find something to eat.

The installation suggested that work made people's faces bleed.

Cheryl liked her job, which took place in a cube, overseeing projects for the city government. Her latest task was to manage the engineering of artificial light for the parks department. Light and parks made people happy, and she was particularly proud because the artificial lights had been her idea. The last thing she wanted was a head wound.

She didn't believe that cubicles killed people. These people were already dead, she thought, before they'd even gotten into the elevator. Each corpse in the installation had desk photographs of miserable looking toddlers throwing balls, climbing on furniture, or torturing pets. Children were the real killers.

Once through the exhibit, they retreated to the quiet second floor, vaulted and church-like, and lost themselves in the galleries. They walked aimlessly among the endless portraits with placards identifying only the artist and date of the painting. Here, they looked at each enormous, brown portrait or landscape, and pondered it for three to four seconds before moving on without the pressure of feeling like they had to learn something. Cheryl liked not being told what to think, though here she could use some help: was this all they had to offer them, these dark halls of excess? She felt like they were browsing the vault of a bank.

The museum reminded her of Tammers' apartment. Tammers had made a small fortune after college when she'd invented a phone application that allowed users to make anonymous, three-second videos of themselves that were added to a collage of other, randomly selected three-second user videos. The application was a huge sensation for those looking to create real connections with people all around the world.

With her new money, Tammers retired and moved into a cavernous condo near the top floor of an architecturally significant building designed as a holding place for the storage of excess capital. What Tammers had purchased was unfinished space with concrete walls, rough floors, and plywood furniture. She liked the coldness of the space and its simulated furniture.

In the corner of a dim corridor, Tammers stopped them in front of a small oil-on-wood panel of a girl and her dog, a sort of primitive, proto-cocker spaniel. Tammers' dog had been a cocker spaniel too, and Cheryl thought the dog was a dead-ringer for Mr. Slippers, though somewhat wider and wild. Tammers looked at the painting longer than any other painting in the museum, but she didn't reach for her phone. Instead, it looked as if she was trying to conjure the kind of sadness she thought should have been provoked by suddenly seeing the image of her beloved dog emerge in the darkness of a museum hallway from the ethereal light of a small, minor oil painting.

The eyes, Cheryl thought. *The dog's eyes.*

She understood exactly what Tammers was going through. Cheryl slid her hand into Tammers' hand. She was in the process of realizing in a new way that her best friend was gone and Cheryl wanted to be supportive.

Tammers shrugged. She looked at her phone.

"I'm thirsty for a Julius," she said. "I wish the mall hadn't burnt."

They decided to drive to Tammers' condo, where Tammers felt she might be able to make them Orange Juliuses from scratch, though Cheryl was skeptical because Tammers had neither a refrigerator nor a blender. Tammers promised her, so she agreed.

In the basement, they walked back through the contemporary gallery on their way to retrieve their coats and paused again to try to find something in the art they'd come to see. Cheryl thought of the mall, the things on display, and the desire she sometimes felt in the Bon-Ton, watching Tammers try on tracksuits or a marked-down dress. She could have those things, could understand them.

Cheryl stopped in front of a small painting, barely larger than a notebook page, a landscape of a dead farm with a feeble, purple horse grazing in a sterile field. Something about the purple horse activated a kind of feeling in Cheryl's stomach, a feeling like hunger and pain, a longing for something she had not known she wanted. She tried to conjure an articulation of this new feeling, like an awareness of something long lost.

Next to her, an unattended child stood in front of a large landscape, a smudge of purple and yellow and bright green at the foot of majestic slate-gray mountains. The child had pushed his entire hand into his mouth and saliva drooled out around the perimeter of the boy's wrist.

She looked back at the painting in front of her and waited to feel the new feeling she had felt, but now the painting was just a painting.

A crack sounded somewhere in the wall of the gallery.

The child pulled his hand out of his mouth and pressed his sopping palm against the canvas, then he moved his hand like a brush in a broad sweep across the painting. He smiled. The painting, at last, was finished.

"Hey, step back!" A guard yelled, running toward the child.

Another crack, louder, from above them.

The guard grabbed the child's arms, pulled them behind the child's body, and secured them with zip ties. The guard, having touched the boy's hands, thick with saliva, looked as if he might vomit.

"Cheryl, I'm ready to go." Tammers hovered behind her.

"Just another minute," Cheryl said. "I'm feeling something."

Tammers snorted.

The boy began to scream. A rasping, like the bending of metal, echoed through the gallery. The museum visitors paused, looking away from the art on the walls and to the ceiling and floor, looking for the source of the sound.

Someone shrieked as a pool of brown water surged across the museum floor. The foul water, like sewage, covered the bottoms of their still-wet feet, and quickly reached their ankles, soaking into their shoes and socks and the bottom of their jeans. An alarm howled, and a voice on the intercom, hard to hear over the noise, said something about evacuating.

"This is not a test," came through clearly.

The guard, struggling to take the child somewhere, perhaps to an undisclosed interrogation room, left the boy alone with his arms zip-tied behind his back, and ran toward the door, dropping his badge on the ground behind him.

The visitors moved like they were stuck in a chaotic current, bouncing around each other with no idea where to go. Some of them pointed to a glowing exit sign leading them away from the filthy, wet floor, and together they swarmed forward, pushing into one another as if their lives were in danger.

"Please move carefully to the nearest exit," the voice said over the intercom. "This is not a test."

Cheryl took Tammers by the hand and together they joined the river of people trying to get out, pausing to help a toddler who had stumbled, a toddler whose mother had pushed ahead of her, leaving her to fend for herself.

"Do not use the revolving doors," the voice said. "Do

not trample one another."

Cheryl remembered a horrific accident years ago in which an evacuation of a high rise hotel had led to people getting crushed in the revolving doors as people desperate to escape pushed forward despite others trying to exit. The door became jammed with bodies, and the survivors inside waited nearly two hours, bodies piled upon bodies, while rescuers freed them.

"I can't leave without my raincoat," Tammers said. She pointed to the coat check.

Volunteers helped the suddenly swamped attendant find people's coats and bags, repeating "we need to get out of here," but still dutifully attending to people's outerwear.

"I'm not going down with the ship," the attendant said, jumping over the counter and rushing toward the door.

A security guard told them to leave their belongings; the water was coming in fast and they didn't know if the ceiling would hold, but there they waited, the water rising.

The smell of the museum's shit engulfed them. Tammers began to cry. She whispered to Cheryl that she missed her dog, that she could feel him still, in her arms, and that she did not really believe he had died, but was instead taken away from her. At night, she could hear his claws scratching on the cold concrete floors. She begged to no one for his return, her pleas echoing through her enormous, empty apartment.

Cheryl put her arm around Tammers and they pushed through the crowd to the front of the coat check line. Tammers sobbed, convulsive and gulping, into her arm.

"Please, we need our coats," she said to nobody in

particular. "It's an emergency."

A HUNGER

Rebekah Bergman

A HUNGER

Rebekah Bergman

My mother—more than once I caught her standing dead center in a department store, arms by her side empty, head tilted up into the too-bright light.

My sister is the same way, yearns only to be low-maintenance, answers "I don't care. What do you want?" again and again. At restaurants, I order for her. I say "She's going to have" and not "She'd like."

I have a son at home. The boy can jump from the living room to the dining room in a single bound. He wears all his lucky shirts at once, layer atop layer. A commercial plays, and he says "Oh. Can I please have that? I have been wanting that all my life."

When food is placed before my sister, she moves a tired face close to it, frowns down, as if this meal is her reflection, and she should not have hoped for anything more. "That," I say, "looks delicious."

I feed my son milk for his bones and carrots for his eyesight. I feed him chocolate as a reward for cleaning his room. He eats it all and asks for seconds. If any remains, he can take thirds. I do not say my son is insatiable. I say he is hearty. I say his body is growing to be healthy and strong.

As children, we faced the yearly question of our mother's birthday. What should we get her? What did she want, this mother who did not have a favorite child because she did not have a favorite anything at all?

One year, my sister suggested a Gameboy. "She wants to play it with us," she said, and I was convinced. We shoveled snow for the neighbors. We saved our lunch money. We walked the one large dog that lived down the block. We chose the green Gameboy and wrapped it in blue paper with a silver ribbon. It looked real, like an actual gift. I don't remember what our mother did when she opened it. If her face fell. If we felt guilt.

There is a folktale that my son knows from preschool and is still scared of. A queen transgresses by eating what she is not meant to eat: an onion, the skin and all, layer atop layer. She becomes a witch. She births a son. The witch who was a queen and becomes a mother, she sees her new son and feels inside her a monstrous hunger.

She looks at the boy who emerged from her body.
    She says, "I want to bite and chew you."
    She says, "I want to eat you up."

I AM ME

Kevin Finucane

I AM ME

INNOVATIVE SHORT FICTION CONTEST WINNER

Kevin Finucane

Upstairs. The Lapsteins were at it again. Lin set her spoon on the table and waited patiently for what would come next.

The awkward pounding escalated in tempo and gave way to the telltale sound of wood snapping and bodies collapsing to the floor. Lin had long grown accustomed to the Lapstein's lovemaking and the shattered remains it left behind. Given the splintering sound and immediacy of the fall, Lin was quite sure the victim this time was the sun-bleached coffee table Mr. Lapstein had hauled into their building just yesterday.

Now, its future was all but written. Like the tables before it, it will be pushed out the window in the general direction of the dumpster. The Lapstein's children, god knows how many, will leap gleefully down the fire escape to dismember what hasn't already been obliterated by the fall. The boys will assault each other with the table's torn limbs, some of the girls will egg them on from the sidelines, others will brazenly join the fight until Mrs. Lapstein says "Knock it off" and flicks down the butt of her cigarette for them to wrestle over.

Lin picked up her spoon just as a fist-size chunk of

plaster broke away and crashed inches away from her untouched breakfast—a slice of pink grapefruit, its fleshy segments now spoiled by plaster dust.

Such was the price of living below the Lapsteins.

The Lapsteins moved into The Manchester three years ago for one reason: no background checks. Of course, Mr. Lapstein was seen touring the occupancy with the building's superintendent as if the condition of the place mattered. He waived his long uneven arms at the dings on the walls and water stains on the ceiling. His ropes of knotted hair shook in disappointment at the outdated appliances and the loose curtain rod above the claw foot bathtub. Seeing the superintendent grow impatient, he scribbled his name on the lease as if it were just another credit card slip.

Moments later Mr. Lapstein was seen unpacking a rusty station wagon while Mrs. Lapstein, an athletic-bodied woman with platinum short hair and a dark pinstriped suit, blew smoke rings and talked loudly on her phone about a rash.

There wasn't much to see. Everything the Lapsteins owned was packed in black garbage bags. That is, until one ripped open and released, among other curiosities, a bejeweled undergarment of sorts that took flight in the air with a passing dump truck.

The last thing to be unloaded was an eager-faced boy with a fist-full of chalk. Mrs. Lapstein plucked him out herself like a stray seed. Many more children, all brothers and sisters, would appear out of thin air in the months after. The Lapsteins didn't follow any rules, including the laws of nature.

Lin skipped breakfast. She checked the mirror in the bath before heading to work. A little plaster dust had settled on her knotted bun of black hair. She approved. It imparted a hint of grey. She liked appearing older than twenty and often wore long, woven dresses in various shades of brown. She wanted to be seen as a Korean woman who unabashedly clung to the traditions of her homeland. It was an image only she saw. The bluntness of her nose and blue eyes announced a more mixed heredity.

Before landing the job at Paris Nails up in Manhattan, Lin spent a few days behind the counter at the Mobile. Nothing delighted a New Yorker more than hearing a southern drawl out of an Asian woman. "That's *oil* not *erl*, Linda," her boss laughed in an accent she couldn't place. It's not that she was ashamed of how she talked. She didn't see the point conversing for the sake of conversing. But like eye contact and empathy, these were the things she must learn if she ever wanted to complete the *I Am Me* program. So said her sponsor, Mitch, a freckled-face kid who turned to knitting his own clothes. Without the certificate of completion, she could kiss her grant money behind. And without college, Lin thought, she might as well be her mom.

"You ready for Thanksgiving?" Mrs. Bishop asked, sitting down at Lin's table for her biweekly manicure at Paris Nails. Mrs. Bishop was a regular. Not because Lin was especially good at giving manicures or because Paris Nails had anything in the way of amenities, but because Mrs. Bishop could ramble on about her life without becoming part of the gossip column in her Upper East Side salons.

"Thanks for giving?" Lin cocked her head slightly over her lamp.

"No. *Thanksgiving*. You know, family gathers. Eats turkey. Everyone grateful that they don't have to do it again for another year."

"Thank you for coming today," Lin said, appearing proud at her ability to say an entire phrase in English.

"No dear. It's a holiday. Indians and Americans make friends. Eat turkey. Understand?"

"Grandmother make Turkey soldier in war."

Once Mrs. Bishop was convinced that Lin had made little progress in the way of fluency, she would start talking, usually about her husband's ongoing affairs. She prided her knack to pit one mistress against the other.

Preston was careless. His iPhone was often left out and unlocked. His calendars and messages were without code or discretion, as were the names of his various accounts and handles — *fitfiftyforfun* — *toofastforlove* — all in the name of the cash-strapped college dropouts he'd pick up online.

Or Preston wasn't careless. He needed help shedding the girls he'd become tired of. When Mrs. Bishop first caught on to her husband's adulterous ways, she would only send tastefully written messages revealing trysts planned by competing mistresses. But she found this digital communication far too impersonal. It lacked quality, a sense of something earned and expended, which is how Mrs. Bishop turned to flower delivery instead. Nothing left an impact more on Preston's women or his bank account than receiving an extravagant bouquet of flowers from his wife.

Dearest Laurel — Congratulations on your recent internship inside my husband's pants. He's also screwing your roommate, Stacey, this very moment on the north side of your fourth-floor parking garage. Hugs, Mrs. Bishop.

"Now he's got a young one in the ranks. Kaitlyn's her name," Mrs. Bishop continued. "A full two years younger than our own daughter, mind you. I'm sending the lot of them a Tuscan orchid and an invitation to meet at his little loft on Tuesday. They may be floozies, but at least they're self-policing."

Lin had learned to smile like the other Asian women who work in the salon when they don't understand a word but still want to appear polite to their talkative clientele. The truth was, Lin was raised on tractor pulls and fried chicken just outside of Walterboro, South Carolina.

Lin's mother, Pearl, called between clients. Lin didn't have to look at her phone to know. Pearl was the only one who called. Even if her mother could text, Lin's new phone couldn't support it. Lin was restricted to voice calls. No Internet. Nothing. Texting initiates the user checking habit. The checking habit reinforces short duration habitual usage. Short duration habitual usage, her sponsor Mitch informed her, was bad. It was the gateway to media appetency. Unhealthy social intercourse. Dissociative identities. Longer duration habitual usage. All in all, the reason she had to drop out of NYU.

"Now where you calling from?" Lin whispered in the break room, which doubled as the storeroom and employee toilet.

"Where love comes too soon, and leaves too late. You got a boyfriend yet, or whatever? I'm the last to judge. Who needs grandchildren? Too many mouths. Too many assholes when you get right down to it."

"I told you not to call when you've been drinking."

"Ha! You call *this* drinking?"

Lin went back to work. Nicki was waiting for her behind a towering cup of Starbucks smeared with lipstick.

"You like living in New York?" Nicki asked, pushing her hands into Lin's. "In the big city, that is. I don't mean *here* here. I want to live in the country."

Nicki's hands shook. She said she took prescriptions to help her feel balanced, although they sometimes made her feel small. She practiced veganism in fits and starts. She could eat all day, she whispered, if not for the messiness of what would happen afterward. She never used a public toilet—not once—she said.

"Ever been to Clinton? It's the best. I have an aunt there. She has a private guesthouse. We could go sometime," Nicki's eyes darted as if blinded by a reflection. "So do you like living in the city?"

"Yes. It likes me."

"Lin," Nicki whispered cautiously over the table, "a Korean wouldn't say 'It likes me' instead of 'I like it.' Not very convincing, unless you are trying to pass yourself off as a Latina. Come on, I've been on to you for months."

"Latina? Teacher Latina."

"Not a good save." Nicki's fingers stroked Lin's wrist. "We're all just pretending. Or are we? Let me buy you a latte. You're definitely a latte. I knew the first time I saw you. Extra froth. Brilliant."

"Relax," Lin said, massaging the tension from Nicki's hands. "Close your eyes."

Nicki obeyed and before long she was murmuring absentmindedly. She imagined her fingers were slices of sponge cake and that Lin was nibbling them off, one by one, stopping between mouthfuls to wipe the crumbs off her delightfully exposed breasts.

▪   ▪   ▪

Next morning, whistles rang from above as Lin stepped out of The Manchester, followed by a chorus of girls' voices belting, "Good morning Mrs. Lin!"

Three identical Lapstein girls with flat faces were huddled together on the third-story window ledge. Their feet dangled and clapped below. A single strand of red ribbon ran through their blond curls, tethering them together. They giggled as their heads clunked one after the other.

"Shouldn't you be in school right now?" Lin asked, as if they had met before.

"Sorry about your ceeeeeeeeeeeeiling!" They raised their clasped hands and leaned forward as if to leap off the window's ledge. Laughing, they kicked up their white stocking legs instead and fell backward through the window curtain.

"About the other day," Lin's mother, Pearl, mumbled into the phone.

"That was yesterday."

"Will you stop attacking me? As if you ever were able to see anything through, yourself, you know?" Pearl took a long drag from her cigarette. "Tell me about school. How do you get money? I'm your mother, I should know."

"Computer science. I'm a prostitute."

"So you *do* like men!"

Lin can't tap into her grant money again until she successfully completes Offline Support, a critical stage of the *I Am Me* curriculum. The acquisition of real-life friends and activities are said to deter habitual online behaviors. Lin was falling behind. She hadn't made friends at the required socials. No one felt real, especially herself. During a game of Monopoly, Mitch stopped her from poking a stupid girl in a pink wig with her nail file. Lin had wanted to see if she would bleed.

The bus stopped out front of Paris Nails. Lin watched with some interest as Scott jumped off. He came in every other week to get the acrylics on his right hand repaired and shaped. Long nails are essential, he had informed Lin, if you want to crush the trachea with any expediency.

"I picked up a good one last night," Scott said sitting down at Lin's table. "She was working East 9th in a yellow spandex jumpsuit so tight that you could see her soul ripple and dip with every step. You like dark meat, Lin?"

Lin smiled and picked up her nail file.

"Anyways, got real feisty after I got her back in my apartment. Took a good three minutes for her to drop. I cracked the nail on my index. See?"

"Usual?" Lin asked nodding her head toward his right hand.

"Yes. So, can I start keeping some product in your freezer? I've run out of space in mine. I'll pay you in barbeque. Carolina-style, I presume?"

Scott claimed to spend his nights slaying streetwalkers because of their distinctive flavor and abundance, but Lin pegged him right away for a classical guitarist. He was fussy about how his nails were shaped and always wore protective gloves.

"Look, we can stop the act," Scott said. "I've seen you read through the headlines across the street. Your English very good. Better than mine, I bet. Let's grab a drink sometime. I won't eat you."

Lin smiled, as if she had been listening the entire time. She hadn't. She had been mentally checking-in on her online profiles. It was common among habitual users, even reformed ones, Mitch lamented, to engage apps and identities without a device. "Relevancy decay is a process," Mitch said while knitting furiously away on a pant leg.

What if our digital selves inhabited the entire city, Lin thought, a city bustling with our self-renditions? And when users, like herself, fell absent or were required to deleted their accounts for the sake of higher education, their online profiles lived on and bettered themselves without further input. It was a crazy thought. But it made Lin smile as she grabbed her nail pliers and twisted off a broken tip from Scott's ring finger, careful to disguise her exhilaration as he winced in pain.

Lin came home that evening to find a few Lapsteins out front of The Manchester taking turns swinging at a fire hydrant with a hammer.

"Maybe that's not a good idea?" Lin said walking up behind them.

"Can you help us?" the boys asked in unison.

"Eleven! Mind my hammer!" yelled Mr. Lapstein leaning out of their front window wearing nothing but boxer shorts and body hair.

"Hello Ms. Lin," said a little voice behind her. "I'm Nineteen." She turned around to find a young dark-skinned girl in orange curls and a green painting smock. "I got chalk. See?"

She grabbed Lin's hand and led her around to the back of The Manchester. "The older boys are always trying to ruin my contrivances."

"Contrivances?"

The girl drew a boy with shaggy hair, overalls and a Yankee's hat into a patch of cement behind the trash bins.

"Stay still," Nineteen commanded as she drew the boy's face.

"Is the nose a little crooked?" Lin asked, touching her own.

"It's not *your* nose. I'm just taking your eyes. He's

going to be my little brother."

"He ain't ready yet," said an older girl spying from the fire escape. "He got no hands. Remember what happened to Fifteen."

"Wasn't me." Nineteen insisted before adding a set of hands. "What about you Ms. Lin, what's been forgotten on you?"

"Nothing," Lin said, ignoring the pang in her chest.

"Something's missing on your insides," the girl replied.

Lin looked away.

"Don't make you less real," Nineteen added, as if she was sorry she said anything at all. "You just need to let yourself fill out, normal like, is all."

Lin had spent years developing her twelve identities on Facebook and other social media. Each one bore images she lifted online of possible pets, vacations, family, food and passions. They were trial runs of what she could be, permeations of o`thers she developed until they felt familiar. She sorted through friends like playing cards. Every like and dislike, every post strategic. Before having to give it all up, Lin was certain that if she distilled these twelve down to one profile, she would know who she ought to be. Mitch said she would just turnout like everyone else, as if there was no alternative.

▪   ▪   ▪

"How many husbands do you know get to have a focus group for their cock?" asked Mrs. Bishop the next morning, her gin and tonic still audible.

"Fill or full-service?"

"Exactly. He had a good thing." Mrs. Bishop dropped

an open-toe Chanel on Lin's table. "Color nails same, please."

"Gold?"

"Guess how much these shoes cost," she said leaning in. "I'll tell you. A. Shit. Load. That's the price Mr. Bishop pays when telling his girlfriend he loves her."

"Give it time." Lin said, giving the empathy thing a spin.

"So now you give marital advice, huh?"

"I make nails pretty."

"That's better."

Lin was ready to call it a day when Scott jumped through the door and unleashed his dark curls from a black hoodie. The other technicians filed out behind him for the evening. If they hadn't already pegged Lin as an undercover immigration agent, they might have had concern for her safety.

"I used to brine the meat first," Scott said, giving Lin his right hand. "You have to with lean meats. But it added a day to the process. Now I just use all that brining time to cook the meat at lower temps for longer periods. That's the trick with good barbecue, you go slow and low. And if it's a hair dry at the end, slather it with sauce."

"New?" Lin asked. It had been hardly twenty-four hours since he was in last, but his nails looked butchered.

"Yes. There was this tribe in the South Pacific that ate their enemies to help them be stronger in battle. They also found it made them perform better in the sack. Eh? In any case, the tribe they fought against lived on an island just a short paddle away. This other tribe ate their enemies for an entirely different reason. They didn't want the souls of their adversaries to have bodies to torment them in the afterlife. Remarkable, isn't it? To have two tribes with such disparate beliefs living so close to each other? Anyways, we all have different reasons for why we consume people. Flesh or not, it doesn't change our diet. And yet here you go, doing my nails every week, acting like I don't exist. What if I did?"

"Keep still," Lin said holding his hand down and reaching for her nail pliers. He must have had a performance last night, Lin reasoned, cutting off his shattered tips. Notice the small things. Listen relentlessly. Be your Self. The *I Am Me* mantras rose in her thoughts like weeds after rain. Lin had asked Mitch, her sponsor, to tell her about his Self, because she was pretty sure he didn't have one. He said stop reading into it. It just meant she needed to be out in the world—without us, without anyone—alive and breathing. Just know, he added, real people suck.

"Lin, what are you hiding from?" Scott said. "C'mon. Just one drink with me. Loosen up."

"This hurt?" Lin asked, prying off a damaged tip.

"Yes. It wasn't so long ago scientists believed cannibalism was caused by having a bad humour lodged in one's heart."

Lin smiled her same smile until Scott was done and out the door. She stepped up to the window to watch him walk down the sidewalk. She tried to imagine herself introducing him as a friend at the next *I Am Me* social. He would think she was ridiculous, she worried.

"I want to unwrap you," Nicki said, popping out of the darkness and pushing through the door before Lin had a chance to lock it. "You're not somebody's byproduct."

"Closed now." Lin said.

Nicki sat down anyway. "I want to take away your worries. Strip you down so you can breathe again and be free from fear, or whatever it is that makes you hide. I can't stop thinking about it. Come over tonight."

"Late now. Must go," Lin said.

"You are worried. You saw the news about the missing woman. You are scared, yes? I'll come to your apartment."

"Husband home," Lin said looking up at the clock.

"You're not married," Nicki said louder than she should have and grabbing Lin's hand. "I know a lot about you, Lin. I know you are lonely. I know you speak and write English very good. I know that you are scared of your body, of sex, of defecation and the mask you wear. You need me to release you."

Lin pointed to the security camera, "Yes. Release you. Go now, come tomorrow."

Nicki bent her knees and shrieked with anticipation before collecting herself out the door. Lin opted to walk back instead of taking the bus. The thought that she could be in mortal danger excited her. She imagined a masked man leaping out at every turn from the shadows. And then what? He would reach for her throat, throw her to the ground. She would wake up in a basement somewhere.

But then her mother called.

"I'm coming to New York for Thanksgiving. To be with you, of course," Pearl said. This statement was followed by a description of the phone she was calling from, the ridiculous tongue-ring worn by a rude barman at a reception she crashed, more details about the phone, but none about the phone's owner, a man who said his name was Don in the background, but who Pearl kept referring to as Doug.

"You can't come here. I don't have furniture. You know gambling is illegal in New York?"

"If you got room for your Johns, you got room for

us. Look, we don't care if you like girls. Doug thinks it's kinda cool. What do you mean, there's no casinos in New York?"

It was late by the time Lin made it back to The Manchester. Mr. and Mrs. Lapstein were already in full swing upstairs. Their porcelain tub moaned as their limbs sought traction and points of leverage on its slippery surface. Lin undressed and sat on the toilet, naked and feeling completely comfortable with her body—despite what Nicki liked to think. The gasps above fell into a familiar staccato.

She imagined their entangled bodies mashing in clumps of body hair, their open mouths devouring each other's bruised skin. She thought about Mr. Lapstein plunging haphazardly away like some lost rodent trying to make its way through a dark and unforgiving maze.

Lin's showerhead rattled. She knew they were close.

Lin pressed her fingers inside herself with the same clumsy vigor. She imagined what her own insignificant body looked like from above, legs splayed open over the toilet seat and narrow abdomen heaving like a spider being sucked into a vacuum. She wanted to be consumed. She wanted to release. Why not? The thought of coming with them excited her. And when they eventually did, she was showered in plaster and rotten wood.

. . .

"You alright, ma'am?" a boy's voice called over to her the next morning. Lin had taken the back exit out of The Manchester, hoping to not run into any Lapsteins. "You looked out of sorts last night."

"Just startled a bit," Lin said into the alley, not seeing

where the voice was coming from. "Wasn't expecting a bathtub to go through my ceiling, is all."

"Kinda frozen there for a spell," the boy said. Lin saw him laying down in the very spot Nineteen had drawn him. He had a crooked nose and wore overalls and a Yankee hat. His face had a grey hue that matched the cement around him.

She recalled seeing him in the flesh for the first time the night before. She opened her eyes up after the crash to find the bottom of the clawfoot tub suspended above her and a half dozen Lapsteins peering through the open ceiling.

"Isn't it dangerous to be laying down in the alley? A car might not see you."

"Wanted to see if I grew is all," he sat up. The chalk drawing underneath him was already worn by tire marks.

"Your name?"

"Twenty," yelled Nineteen from the fire escape. "He's only couple days old and ain't got no sense yet."

"You were something to see," Twenty said grinning.

Lin went to work.

"So. That's that," Mrs. Bishop said, "Preston left me for a younger woman, one nourished by organic quinoa and built for yoga and fucking. But let's not be petty, Kaitlyn holds an excellent position over at the Whole Foods off 14th, a floor trainer of some kind, and claims to have no aspirations to acquire wealth. She told Preston to leave me the bank account, the club membership, and the house. Very considerate of her. Makes me almost regret maxing his credit cards these past few days. Almost. She didn't tell him to give up his salary, of course, or his stocks, or our beach house in Montauk which will be perfect, she says, for hosting workshops on sustainable living.

That's her niche, Preston said, minimal impact. Twit. And won't you believe it? Some of the other members of his former flock have been rather sympathetic to my plight and curious themselves on how this most abnormal of affairs will play out. We've even started our own blog, thewomenwhosleptwithprestonbishop. It has been a nice way to vent, for all of us really, as well as connect again. It's artificial, I know, but it's a small step toward some kind of healing. Oh, I do miss the game though. I miss working them all into a dither. Isn't nostalgia disgusting? It's the first indication of getting old, dear. Remember that. People from your part of the world never look old though. You all age gracefully. Preston probably would have liked you. In fact, I know Preston would have liked you. Missed that ship, dear. Now look at you, sitting here doing my nails, pretending you don't understand a word I'm saying."

Lin smiled politely.

"But let's say you didn't miss the ship," Mrs. Bishop said quietly. "Let's say you do understand what I'm saying, and I offer you a lot of money, enough for you to take a long, long visit back to wherever you came from. And the only thing you had to do was sleep with my husband?"

"I make pretty," Lin said, grabbing Mrs. Bishop's hands and reaching for her nail pliers. She imagined Mrs. Bishop's creased-filled pinky snapping off effortlessly under the tempered steel blades.

"Visually speaking," Nicki said sitting down at Lin's table an hour later, "I prefer the dorsal versus the palmer aspect of the hand, don't you? The palm is profane, especially when exposed upward in supplication, as if forgiveness were an option."

Flecks of Rouge 999 lacquer flickered on Nicki's teeth. She had been fidgeting outside the salon taking large gulps of coffee, pounding on her mobile, and chewing on her nails until Mrs. Bishop, appearing especially pleased with herself, left. "New color today?" Lin asked.

"I must see you tonight." Nicki whispered, inserting a piece of paper into Lin's hand and holding it closed. "Did you know that the fingertips contain the densest areas of nerve endings in the body? Of course you did."

"No," Lin said, trying to withdraw her hand gently from Nicki's grasp. Lin wasn't ready. Being touched was not part of the *I Am Me* program, a fact Mitch disputed.

"That's what got me thinking," Nicki said, eyes darting as if chasing a fly. "For someone so disconnected, you spend a lot of time holding hands. You listen with such avid disinterest—I think you rely on every word. That's it, isn't it? You need us. You would shatter to pieces without us."

Lin had to let go. Not just of Nicki, she was realizing, but all of them. She had to go offline, really offline, once and for all.

Nicki closed her eyes and squeezed harder. "And here I sit fully prepared to make you whole, except—I will be the one who falls apart as soon as you—as you—release—"

"Release my hand, Nicki," Lin said, breaking character. "I'm not sure I like this." Nicki slid down in the chair and pushed her knee deep in between Lin's legs.

"As soon you—as you—oh, god." Nicki moaned, her eyes open and welled pleadingly, "Don't hold back."

"Please," Lin said, relaxing her legs. She brought down the flat edge of her file against Nicki's knuckles. It wasn't as hard as she could have. So she did it again. And then, again. "Let go."

"I am. I am—" Nicki said deflating into the chair.

A wave of wearied commuters spilled out of the bus in front of the salon. Scott ran in just as Lin was raising the file for the fourth time. Nicki and Lin's faces were flushed.

"She's in love with you," Scott said after Nicki left, hardly composed. "She's been spying on you for awhile."

He picked up Nicki's address off the table and held it up for Lin.

· · ·

Lin left Scott sitting at her table without so much of a goodbye. She splurged for a cab. She needed a moment to breathe. That was not going to happen. Her phone kept ringing. Pearl wasn't settling for voice mail.

"We're just staying for a few days, or so. Think how many years I had to put you up," her mother said.

Before Lin could protest, the cab pulled in front of The Manchester and was met with a loud bang. It could have been a gunshot.

Lin jumped out and found Twenty and Fifteen hiding behind a panel truck.

"Watch out, Ms. Lin," giggled Twenty. He lit a large firecracker for his brother to kick into the street toward a passing city bus.

"Do you have a lighter?" Fifteen asked, "Ours about out." His arms fidgeted under his sweatshirt like trapped wings.

Lin shook her head. "Did you ask your mother?"

"She keeps it out of reach," Twenty said, twirling a piece of chalk in his hand. "For now," he added, nodding to the entrance of The Manchester.

Twenty had sketched a girl on the stoop. She wore a thick set of glasses and shared Fifteen's round face and Twenty's crooked nose. Her small mouth, barely a line, was solemn in contrast to her bright red freckles and happy coils of hair. And then there were the legs. They were unruly. They descended all the way down the steps ending in small balloons at the bottom.

"We want a sister," Fifteen said.

"But not the tattletale kind," Twenty added.

. . .

The next morning Lin woke to the pungent smell of roasting meat, something akin to beef or pork. She didn't bother getting dressed to investigate, half expecting Scott to be in her kitchen leaning over the stove basting a limb. But the apartment was empty. She felt an absence, or what others might call loneliness, and dismissed it. She just needed to wake up, she thought, stepping into her shower and turning on the cold water.

"That's some fine smelling meat," whispered a voice.

The Lapstein's tub no longer dangled through the ceiling, but the hole was still there just the same. The red freckled girl with springy hair had no problem sticking her head and shoulders through. Her thick glasses greatly magnified her eyes, making Lin feel as though she were a specimen under a microscope.

"Where did you come from?" Lin asked.

"The front stoop. Last night I felt myself take shape in all that chalk. And look, here I am," she said matter-of-factly. "About that pot outside your door. Some of us were tempted to open its top and pick at the meat all morning while you slept. Not saying that's what my brothers are doing. I, myself, thought it would be prudent to ask first."

"I'm a vegetarian," Lin replied, lying. "You can have the whole pot—if you teach me how to draw."

"Deal." The girl said dangling an arm through the hole. "I'm Twenty-One."

Lin wasn't two steps out of The Manchester when a black sedan pulled up with a gold and diamond-studded hand jutting from the window to beckon her closer.

"Let me give you a lift," Mrs. Bishop said. "I think you will appreciate the arrangement I have for you."

"Thank you. No."

"I have your entire life, right here." Mrs. Bishop held up a folder. It was thin. Lin kept walking. "Okay. So it's a bit dry, but you should know there's someone creeping around your apartment and talking to those kids. Pictures to prove it." Lin stopped and got in.

Once they pulled up to Paris Nails, Mrs. Bishop tried to give Lin something like an embrace before she stepped out. Lin wouldn't have it. "You don't actually have to sleep with Preston," Mrs. Bishop said. "Just muddy the waters between him and his little floor trainer. Now don't make that face. It's the best for all concerned, including you."

The salon was quiet for once. A yellow goldfish hovered alone in a leaky aquarium and watched the puddle below it expand across the dirty linoleum. An idle technician sat with her head bent thumbing away on her phone. It had been ninety-seven days since Lin had updated a profile, much less held a device capable of doing so. She didn't feel liberated, though. She felt only waiting. As if she were part of something bigger that wouldn't let go.

"You aren't real," Scott said, sitting down at Lin's table. "You don't have any friends. The only person who calls you is your mother, who you lie to. You live off of beef jerky and grapefruit. Your phone can't even take a text message. You have no digital footprint. I am not sure you have a real footprint, actually. I bet you don't have a single photograph, keepsake, past due bill, or anything in your apartment that says, I exist in this world."

Lin smiled. "New nails today?"

"Listen for once," Scott said reaching for her arm. "You are surprised about what I know. Nicki was very surprised about how much I knew. You really shouldn't have let me run off with her address. And you really shouldn't have led her on so. She really believed you were a victim of some kind. She had no idea of what you had inflicted upon her, upon all of us. The subtle manipulation, our lives putty in your hands."

The back of Lin's neck grew warm. She grabbed her nail pliers. She didn't understand desperate people, much less how she could be part of anyone else's desperation.

"But I digress," Scott continued, letting her arm go. "What a lovely dinner I had. Nicki was a little wound up, at first, but after learning that she would soon be inside you—well, she seemed to almost melt. How did you like her by the way? A pinch heavy on the cardamom? I found her a little stringy, a quality that plagues leaner cuts. Oh, and don't worry about returning the pot. Might come in handy at your place."

"Well, I guess everyone has a need that not just any *body* will fulfill," Scott went on. "This is your last chance. I'd hate to start cooking your neighbors. Well, hate is a bit excessive. It's a regular veal farm over at The Manchester. Just answer this question: What makes you real?"

"Dinner," Lin said, grabbing Scott's thumb. "Thursday. Seven o'clock. Plenty of fresh product."

Later that afternoon, Mrs. Bishop swung through the door carrying bags from Barney's and a look of victory.

"Preston is excited to meet you," she said, sitting down and presenting her hands. "He didn't say so, of course. But when I told him of a good seamstress, who was young but quite capable—oh, I hope you don't mind that I told him you were a seamstress? Anyway, it'd give him an excuse to come by and drop his pants."

"Full-service?" Lin asked.

"I can't tell you what to do with your body—"

"Nails." Lin lowered her head until her ear pressed against the heat shield of her work lamp. She bit her lip.

"So we have a deal?"

"Thursday. Six forty-five. Cash today."

Lin's lip bled into the afternoon. She had made progress, she thought. Increased social interaction. Diminished reliance on dissociative identities. And now she was well on her way to completing the final stage of *I Am Me*, Offline Support, the acquisition of friends and pastimes. But at what point had she become a prostitute, much less a vegetarian?

"There are things only your mother can provide," Pearl yelled into the phone over a cacophony of slot machines. "And we can't stay in Jersey, so we're coming there. Besides, Doug wants to see what you look like."

"It's Don," Lin corrected. She could remember every one of Pearl's lovers and their lingering hugs. But she won't. "Thursday. Seven o'clock. A minute late and you can forget it."

Lin walked up to find a patrol car idling across the street from The Manchester. Not a Lapstein could be seen. She looked in the basement. A pack of them were in the boiler room taking turns banging on the pipes with a pipe wrench. No sign of Twenty-One anywhere. Fifteen nodded toward the fire escape outside, "She's stealing a smoke."

Lin found her a couple flights up sitting on a handrail coughing through a cigarette. Her long legs reached down nearly a full flight of stairs.

"That's not a good idea," Lin yelled up.

"I'm stunting my growth," Twenty-One mumbled, her small mouth still struggling to catch a breath. From the waist up, she looked hardly nine years old. Her outline still showed chalk marks.

"Could I have your help, inside?"

"In a minute," Twenty-One said, pointing to her cigarette.

"You know. That won't make your legs shorter," Lin said.

"Really?"

"Really."

Twenty-One crept around Lin's apartment hunched over, careful not to take out the ceiling light. She studied the bare walls and the empty shelves as if something ought to belong there.

"No one will play with me except Twenty and Fifteen, and now they're mad at me because I talk too much and won't help them reach stuff we ain't supposed to be reaching."

"Sounds like you could use a friend?"

"Aren't *you* the one who could use a friend, Ms. Lin?" she asked through her curtain of red hair.

"I want you to draw me," Lin said, swallowing the emptiness around her.

Twenty-One, collapsed to the floor and fished out a colorless nub of chalk from her pocket. "It's the last of it.

Daddy hid it in the ceiling light. I want a sister. With legs like mine."

Lin stepped over Twenty-One's legs and gently grasped her hands. She nodded to the bare wall. "We had a deal."

It was late when Twenty-One finished. The resemblance was unnerving with only one exception: the legs. They were still a little long, but Twenty-One was stubborn about having it any other way.

"It's almost midnight," Lin said, looking into her eyes for the first time and seeing somebody who could be a friend. A real friend. "You mother must be worried."

"She don't believe in any worrying or regretting. She says you can't change what you can't change, unless you get caught."

Mrs. Bishop's folder containing the background check she had run on Lin was on the dining table next to her phone. She would leave both behind. The folder didn't contain much of a history, Lin thought, but it was close enough for the new resident to get up to speed. She grabbed her coat and wheeled out her suitcase lined with cash.

"Are you ever coming back?" Twenty-One asked.

Lin smiled. She imagined the moment her doppelgänger would emerge from chalk on the wall and take her first breath. Would this new Lin be scared, unsure who she was or would fall right in, just as the Lapsteins always seem to do?

"I need you to help the new gal get settled?" Lin said, nodding to the folder on the table.

"Guess it would get kinda confusing if you both stuck around," Twenty-One said, looking at her drawing. "I'll wait for her, but I'm going to miss you just the same." She sat up on her knees and blanketed Lin under her red coils until Lin hugged her back.

"Tell your brothers and sisters to stay clear. I've got guests coming over that been known to eat people."

Outside The Manchester, Lin considered her options. College can wait. Everything can wait with the money she had, at least for a year. Lin could start a new life, a new identity, in another city large enough for her to blend in.

The light came on in the Lapstein's place. Fifteen was pressed against the third floor window as if he wanted to pass through it. Lin waived. He hesitated, then stepped back to free an arm from underneath his sweatshirt. He held his wrist up. It was squared off at the top. That's right, she remembered, someone had forgotten to draw in Fifteen's hands. He raised his eyebrows empathetically at Lin as if they shared the some common fate.

Lin could go on just being another profile, living on the wrong side of life. Or she could take a bus south, all the way to Walterboro. She could work the register at the E Z Shop. She could flirt and pour beers at night for the Time Out Sports Bar. She could try doing anything that felt right.

She'll go offline for good, she said out loud. She'll make real friends. She will be somebody. And when she does, she will write Mitch a letter to say that she is the first successful graduate of the *I Am Me* program.

Lin started walking to the subway, her steps powered by a new sense of freedom. She imagined herself, sitting in the first bus leaving that morning, looking through the window at her seat as the bus rolled out of the city. Her face would be beaming through the glass in anticipation of her new life, a real life, as if she really had possessed the power to be free.

TIME TRAVEL

TRAVEL

FOR BEGINNERS

Stephanie Wang

TIME TRAVEL FOR BEGINNERS

Stephanie Wang

The bus is a whale; a wolf; a mechanical Baba Yaga. You ride in its belly, jostled by the other people it has swallowed; too many, in its greed. Beneath your feet its bloated ribcage is cracked, and you press a hand against its steel bones; watch the road trickle past. When it disgorges you onto the street you are pushed through the membrane of rattling doors; licked past its iron teeth; want to gasp at the sudden slap of asphalt and air.

But it passes, onwards and away, and there you are.

It's the same street, and yet. Same same but different. The food vendors you remember have all been moved down side streets, replaced by a square mile of office blocks and slick apartment buildings on the main road. It's a new skin for China, this veneer of late-90s capitalism, but the city's old bones still peek out from beneath. The saplings of your childhood are now brooding leviathans, veining the grey streets with patches of dusky green. The pavement feels gritty beneath your feet. You walk. Memory prickles at your fingers. What do you remember? The roses in the compound across the road, bleeding yellow; still bearing the lovebites of the spring's amorous aphids. The air somersaults about you, smoke-blue, oily, utterly seductive. It presses into you, rubs against your skin like a cat, purrs. You breathe it all in; the cooking smells, the dirty sidewalk, the roses and the heat; you breathe in the sounds, the bicycle bells and the marketeers' cries; the caged larks and finches leading decorative little lives on nearby balconies. The old women, fanning themselves, walking, taciturn; savoring each step in silence like the last vestige of wine in a glass. And they have a story, too; you sense their fear, their regret; the world that is forgetting them by degrees, but the trail twists away; you let yourself be drawn on by the rhythm of your own narrow feet; feel the gravel crunching like the bones of little creatures. Women and men hover like languid flies, conversing, selling; children fling a rubber ball back and forth. A ragged strand of conversation filters back to you and you reach for it; it skirts your comprehension like a cloud of gnats; disperses. This language, it breaks down somewhere between your heart and your lips; it falls in pieces from behind your teeth.

You are a stranger here. Nothing remembers you. You walk. Memory and this, the street; bridged so tenuously; a frail umbilical cord that unfurls. You are lost on your own doorstep; you are Hansel, you are Gretel; you are a girl in red cutting her way through the woods. But old Beijing erodes beneath the new: there is no ancient forest; no witch in its bosky depths, waiting to eat your heart. Not anymore.

As you turn off the last street you catch a glimpse of the temples in the valley below. Poor, forgotten gods. They have died the anonymous death of hermit crabs and snails, leaving behind only their shells. On the road a bicycle repairman sets up an iron picnic on a square of cloth; gestures for you to try his fare. Grease-inked bruises on his face crinkle as he smiles. This man, this ghost in real-time. An impending relic. You shut your eyes, enclose him in the amber of your memory. When he and his ilk disappear from the street, you will know where to find him. You walk.

The heat frays at the edges. Siesta time has ended and as the laneways begin to fill, people brush past; you swing to avoid them. A rickshaw full of scrap metal comes groaning past, cycled furiously by a man in a patchy jacket. He has a voice like a peacock, high and wailing. You walk.

The city flows past you like rain.

The gate you remember is there, unchanged. Bricks of memory harden into life. Iron latch on an iron hinge. Rust grating on rust. You lift, push, walk; you are inside, and there it is; the courtyard and the path; abundantly real. There is the sunburnt door, the barred windows in rows, quaint in their unloveliness. Geraniums nudge the edges of paths, drunk with heat. In the corner, the old sandbox remains. There are children playing there still; a girl in a tartan skirt and a boy with glasses; but that's you and your cousin, isn't it? Because he taught you how to do that; to scratch out a tunnel in a sandhill; and he had you bend your head right down so you could see the light streaming through from the other side. There was a trick to it; the hill couldn't be too high or top-heavy, nor the tunnel too wide, or the whole thing would just collapse. Eventually you became the playground expert on tunnel-digging and moved onto other things, but you won't forget that first morning when you scraped away that last handful of sand; saw the sunlight slicing through its hollow heart. You have never felt that same perfect satisfaction since.

The children in the sandbox keep digging, and you walk into the stairwell. If nuclear war should come to China tomorrow, the cockroaches and that sandbox will remain, ageless, while skeletons of another world crumble around them.

The stairwell is another world too: colder, silent. The railing has been re-painted green. Carelessly. Milky drips on the landing scattered like jewels. The smell of dust, richer than porridge; you taste it as you climb, out of breath, yes; huffing and puffing. You're late. Your hands make ghost prints on the walls. You remember cicadas in the hot Beijing summer; pink flowers hanging from a tree. You remember an ancient sofa, smothered in plastic. You remember the skin on her cheeks like softened soap. You remember legs that failed beneath her. But memory transforms, memory lies. What do you remember? A voice on a phone, but not much else.

On the final landing you stop in front of a newly-painted door. Green. You press a finger against it and some comes away on your skin; tacky, tactile. On the door is a partial fingerprint, a perfect crescent of ridges and tiny lines.

You knock twice.

She who comes through the door is as pale as ricepaper.

She who comes through the door has lips like two goldfish, slippery and red.

She who comes through the door says, hello, hello, I'm sorry I forgot to bring flowers.

She who comes through the door is my lost sun.

She does not change her shoes though I left slippers by the door.

She kisses me hello, hello, grandmother hello.

She takes my old lady hands in hers hello.

These strange words which crackle from her lips like watermelon seeds.

I tell her, Once there was a market, the market of the living. And once there was a market, the market of the dead. Among the dead we waited, and the dead sun glazed our fingers, burned them white as snow.

I tell her, the fox spirits were cunning, and waited until the prince was asleep. Then, quick as midnight, they slipped the scroll from his loosening hands, replacing it with a hollow bone.

I tell her, the young girl wept, and as she cried each bright tear became a crisp bead of jade, and the pigeon said, will you not tell me your troubles, little girl? And the girl said, I weep for I have been cast from my home and have no friends in the world. Then the pigeon dropped a comb of purest pearl into her lap and said, weep no more, child, and together we shall travel this road, and we shall be friends.

I tell her, the wolf smiled, but the woman did not tremble, did not falter. And from the ear of her old grey mare she drew a needle, and this she threw down between them. Instantly there sprang a silver forest, dense with trees as sharp as blades. And she rode on.

I tell her, the prince said, can you forgive me? And the maiden knelt by his sickbed and laid the gold apple by his pillow. In the grey, cheerless room it was like the rising of a small sun, and the perfume that filled the air was richer than butter, sweet as fresh milk. And the prince said, oh, if I could but have one bite of that apple—

I tell her, they are all one; and once they begin, they are all about the way back to the beginning.

What do you remember?

Not much. Not enough. A perfect green crescent, transferred onto the skin. And legs that bent like fishbones. Memory betrays. It isn't enough; it can't hold all that you need it to: all the parables and dying gods and sick roses and the dissolving city. It cannot hold time. The streets blaze into evening: lights on bicycles and cars winking in symphony; neon signs flaring into life; coronas of red and violet mingling in the smog. The air corrosive, corroding. You breathe. You walk. You'll come back.

In the dimly lit sitting room, your grandmother will be leaning back into the sofa amid the squeak and groan of plastic. Rubbing her sinews with failing hands. Her palms will be dry and callused, scratching her calves. Spread across those limbs will be a network of slowly pulsing veins; indigo paths like the roads to Beijing; for the moment, leading home.

MAURICE

Simone Person

MAURICE

Simone Person

Maurice breaks up with you over brunch, citing his commitment issues. He really cares about you, but trying to make a relationship work in a world so full of evil is overwhelming. It's too depressing to be in love, he says. He pays for your Eggs Benedict, drives back to your apartment, gives one last kiss with too much tongue, and says he hopes you find someone who loves you in all the ways he couldn't. Later that week, after you've cried enough to turn the skin around your eyes into crepe paper, ordered daily takeout (which you eat and eat until your stomach cramps in protest), and thrown out everything that reminds you of him—the half-finished tin of smoked almonds, his travel toothbrush festering in your medicine cabinet, the potted succulents you'd named after yourselves—there's a knock at the door.

You look through the peephole and see a woman with hair wild like a clog in a drain holding a silver box. She knocks harder, rattling the doorknob, the hinges. Her bone density must be incredible. A pamphlet slides underneath your door, neon yellow and badly Xeroxed and titled *So, Maurice Finally Ended Things?* You wait until she leaves the box and disappears down the hall before you undo the locks. Maybe it's the food coma or the grief waving over you, but you open the box, don't even check to see if it's ticking or growling. Inside, there's a bag of those liqueur-filled chocolates you love, a baby sloth desk calendar, and the fourth season of *Designing Women* on Blu-ray, which amazes you. You didn't know it was on Blu-ray.

The pamphlet says you're not alone, that people all over the city have been crushed under Maurice's monster truck love. It's not your fault you fell hot and heavy into those big brown eyes. He's just got this way of looking at you that makes your souls feel tethered, we get it. We've been there, him wrapped around us, his lips pressing into that spot underneath our jaw that makes our toes curl. The pamphlet urges you to enjoy the gifts, to pamper yourself in this turbulent time. These items have been carefully selected based on your Internet search history and discarded grocery lists. There's a number to dial if you find it difficult to resist the urge to send him a late-night alcohol-soaked text detailing how much you miss him. It's called The Booty Buster and says volunteers are standing by, waiting to take your call. And there's a support group to meet the other exes, to commiserate and heal. It meets tonight at the YMCA downtown. Refreshments will be provided.

You say, what the hell, and drag yourself out to the meeting. Everyone else is business casual, neatly seated in a semi-circle, ankles crossed one over the other. Little cups of burnt coffee cradled in their hands. You're still in your old college sweatpants, your hair looks weed-whacked, and the stain on your shirt is large enough to raise eyebrows. Their faces are tight with sympathy, and as you walk into the center of the group, tears slipping out, they squeeze your shoulders, rub your back, place their cheeks against yours.

They pull out photos of Maurice, fan them in their hands, showing you his new girlfriend. Han-*nah*, they say, drawing out the second syllable, sneering their faces. A blonde. That's a first, they say. There's rumors of this girl being The One. She's real tight with the mom, they say, the two of them go to brunch without him and order the same thing—Eggs Benedict, light on the hollandaise. They produce charts and PowerPoints and spreadsheets, detailing Maurice's and Han-*nah*'s relationship. High school friends. Went to prom together-but-not-really-together-but-really. Lost touch after her father became convinced another California Gold Rush could happen and moved their entire family to a white flight suburb somewhere outside Oakland. Reconnected in the past month when he ran into her near the bus stop. They spent the evening digging up old memories at a bar downtown. That was the night he called saying he had a stomach bug, that he'd have to cancel your planned *Designing Women* binge-watching extravaganza, leaving you to finish a bottle of wine and most of a Meat Lover's pizza alone.

You want to ask if they traced the last year of your life, collected pictures to angrily gaze over while sipping coffee and drawing Xs across your eyes. Which one was the love of his life before you? And before her? Instead, you ask them to pass you the cookie tray and pick out the walnuts of one as big as your hand, and you watch them pin a betting pool sign-up sheet onto a corkboard wagering when Maurice will break up with her. They ask if you want in, the pot's up to $100, only five bucks to join. You can't see the harm in it, so you pull some crumpled ones from your purse.

They break out the schedule for the following week and offer you a spot. An availability just opened to trail him on his morning coffee run—the last girl decided to go to counseling and move on. She's starting a cupcake business in Fresno with her mom and finishing her nursing degree. They say this shaking their heads, sucking their teeth. The position is yours if you want it. No pay, but the continued existence of this community is pay enough. Didn't the chocolates help you? they ask. What about the sloth calendar? Maurice didn't even remember you liked sloths. He always thought it was ferrets. Maurice used you, like he used us, they say, we're here for you. Warmth spreads through your chest, up your neck, curls around your ears. Taking another cookie, you tell them about your cousin's telescoping camera lens, how she owes you for all those times you bought her cigarettes in high school, and they pencil in your name.

NAMING MAURA MAURA MAURA

Rachel Lyon

NAMING MAURA

Rachel Lyon

Three months into our relationship, many years ago, my wife-to-be grilled me about everyone I'd ever dated. Maybe I whitewashed my past, just a tad. I didn't tell her about my college girlfriend, the French girl, or the neighbor I used to bone. I left out the first girl I dated in the city, who's made no secret of hating me. I told her only about Lydia, my first sweet love, and Maura, who I lived with for three years.

I broke up with Maura in a shitty way. Cheated, lied about it, and eventually disappeared. Moved out one day with no warning, like a coward, while she was at work. I have nothing to say in my defense except: I was in my twenties. I had issues. I've been to therapy since. To my wife I am a better man.

My wife told me about her exes too. I didn't care. My feeling is, in our thirties, baggage is a given. But my wife was a jealous woman. Deep inside her was a hidden pipeline to some poisonous, vindictive waters. She hated my exes. Called them Lydiot and Mauron. I didn't like that, but the name-calling seemed to make her feel better, so I let it go.

She had an awful pregnancy. Sick every day, bedridden for weeks. We needed to laugh. We made up games. Our favorite was What To Name the Baby? We kept a list on the fridge and added to it deliriously. Fluffy. Piglet. Chigger. Stanky Leg. Richard Nixon. The Destroyer. So when one Sunday morning in bed she brought up the name Maura, I thought she was kidding. That's dark, I said. What's dark? she replied.

Coincidentally, it *was* dark. Another thing about her pregnancy was she couldn't sleep. A white noise machine in the corner made white noise. Blackout curtains kept out all the light.

Maura is my ex's name, I said, you know that. She paused to puke a little in the bucket next to the bed. Dutifully I got up to wash it out. I was naked, and as I went into the bathroom, she whistled at me weakly. I just like the name, she said when I lay back down. Her eyes were wide and innocent. She stuck to her guns.

A week or two later, over pineapple pizza and reruns of *House*, she turned to me and said: How about Lydia? Come on, I said. I'm serious, she replied. You're fucking with me, I told her. She said, I don't know what you're talking about. Pregnancy is making you crazy, I said. You've got early onset senility. She said, Don't tell a pregnant woman she's crazy; she'll kill you in your sleep. I took a bite of pizza and looked back at the TV. I said, Hugh Laurie's too good for this show.

She went into labor nearly a month early. It was an ordeal. Lasted thirty-six hours, ended in a cesarean. The baby was the size of a guinea pig with a face like a smashed tomato. My wife—limp hair, damp skin, and broken body—held her tenderly. I was overwhelmed by emotion. The feeling was kind of like: these two creatures, these two beating hearts, these funny-looking hairless bipeds, isn't it crazy, these two are my family. The feeling was like: *Family.* I never understood the word before today. It was like: These two belong to me, and I'll kill you if you so much as touch them. That sounds like anger, maybe, but believe me it was joy.

Then the nurse came in with the paperwork and asked the baby's name, and with the serenity of prayer my wife murmured: Maura.

That snapped me out of it. She's kidding, I told the nurse. She's on multiple drugs.

I'm not kidding, said my wife. Maura. Her name is Maura.

Any parent will tell you their baby is amazing, but Maura is the best. She's fat and happy. Laughs all the time, toothless wheezing and full of glee. We call her Momo or Señora Maura. We hold her upside-down and call her Maur-ova. When we watch TV, we call her Hugh Maurie. When she poops, we say she's left a Mauregon Trail.

Recently, I was pushing her in the stroller when I ran into the original Maura. It's been eight or nine years since we broke up, but still I felt a thrill of regret and desire. She looked good. She'd gained weight. Her hair was longer, lighter. She was walking with another woman, a woman I didn't know.

Well hi, she said. Wow wow wow, I replied. Simultaneously we said: How are you? We gave each other an embarrassed hug while the woman and the baby looked on.

She didn't introduce me to her friend. She knelt down and said, Who's this? The baby did her job and smiled broadly. I gave her a thumbs-up. Good job, kid, I said.

What's his name? she asked. Whose name? I said. She laughed. The baby!

I wanted to use that. I wanted to come up with some little boy's name. We'd been coming up with names for months; how hard could it be? But our list was mostly jokes. I couldn't think of anything except what was still stuck to the fridge. Encyclopedia Brown, I said.

No, really, she said.

Karl Rove, I offered.

Tell me, she said.

I blurted it out. Her name is Maura.

Both Mauras looked up at me. Maura the First said, What? She glanced at her friend, who made a face like, *What a creep!*

Yeah, I said, and shrugged.

The elder Maura stood up. That is super weird, she said.

I should have lied, but it was as if I had forgotten how. So I did the next thing I thought of, which was weirder. Well! I said. Great to see you, Mira!

Mira? she said.

Take care keep in touch! Find me on Facebook! Okay have a great afternoon bye! And, pushing the stroller ahead of me, I hurried away.

That encounter, to be honest, is haunting me. Over the years I've had fantasies about calling up old Maura, telling her sorry for how I behaved years ago. How can I do that now? What would I say? Hey, Mira, remember me? I don't know why I never apologized before, but I can't do it now.

The thing is, though, why would I? That's all in the past. I'm happily married—more happily than ever, now. My relationship with my wife has never been better. Ever since the new Maura, her jealousy has all but evaporated. I have this flirtation with a coworker. It's innocent but years ago would have driven my wife crazy. Now she thinks it's funny. Encourages it, even. It's as if naming Maura Maura plugged up her pipeline to poison with something sweet and good, fat and light. It's as if naming Maura Maura is helping erase the bad man I used to be.

EXTRATERRESTRIAL SCIENCE

J. L. Montavon

EXTRATERRESTRIAL SCIENCE

J. L. Montavon

We had been living in the woods for nearly two years and the food was about to give out when the ship came.

We thought it was a cloud. Clouds foretold our future out here, where only ridges and trees run to the horizon. They told us what mood the gods were in and when they'd unclothe the sun or bring rain to nourish the garden on which so much depended. Clouds were fate, and we were about to discover a new power in them.

Doug ran into our log cabin yelling that something was coming.

"Well, what?" I said.

"It's like—" He sputtered and held his arms wide. "A really weird cloud."

I rolled my eyes at Mary. Doug was the youngest, and we were used to his enthusiasms.

Mother and Father were in the kitchen, which was just a square space in one corner of the cabin, preparing dinner. They didn't even glance our way.

"Hurry!" Doug said.

Mary and I went out. Lisa came running after

us, followed by Jenny the dog. We crowded around Doug at the edge of the clearing that was our camp. He pointed to a spot in the sky above a dust-covered chokecherry bush.

He was right. We'd never seen a cloud like this. Lenticular shapes were normally high in the sky. This one was tilted down and coming toward us.

It got closer and exhaled a big wad of mist. Dusk was falling, and the mist made it hard to see the cloud's features as it hovered above us. It was like a bird diving for prey, yet way bigger and able to slow and hold its position.

"Dinner!" Father called.

We ran inside, terrified. I turned at the door and caught a last glimpse. The cloud seemed solid to me. Usually, they were vaporous, as we saw when they came down and mingled with us in our camp. My mind wrestled with this through the evening.

Lisa tried to describe it to Mother as we sat down to dinner. Father silenced her with a narrowing of the eyes, then looked at me.

"Say the prayer."

I did, and we ate. No one brought up the cloud again. We knew without being told that it was one of those things Father would refuse to acknowledge, like the bears that came snuffling around our camp. His philosophy was: ignore them, and they'll go away. It made us feel the bears wanted something more from us than food, but if we pretended they didn't exist, their desire for whatever it was would evaporate.

That night we got into our sleeping bags in the space, curtained off by canvas, allotted to us in a corner of the cabin.

"It was a ship," I whispered to Mary.

"No. How can that be?"

We keep careful track of the clouds, I explained, to read the temper of the gods, right? Their exhalations flow through the sky above, calm, mischievous, rapacious, angry.

"And?"

"What if the sky is a river of air, like water rivers on land? Couldn't a ship sail to us?"

"The mists around it—they were sails?"

"Unless it uses some kind of propulsion we've never heard of. But I saw it, it gleamed."

"I think I heard it. Not with my ears, but kind of like with my tummy."

"Me, too." Now that I thought about it, I'd felt a low, deep hum in my stomach. It had the feeling of ripples pulsing from inside, as if my stomach was making the hum, not hearing it. "Also, the soles of my feet."

The darkness of the woods filled the room, cut by a few rays of starlight venturing through the window. Mary was a darker shape in the dark in front of me, a long, low ridge of the kind you might see looking out from our camp on a moonless night when the sandman hasn't come, and you've gone outside to wait for him. But I sensed her nod and I heard the change in her breath.

We didn't realize that, despite the softness of my whisper, Lisa and Doug had been listening.

They were full of questions. How can a river be made of anything but water? How can a ship float on air? Why hadn't anyone seen one before?

Mother came and told us to stop talking and go to sleep.

The others did so, judging by their steady breathing. I could not. I stared at the window cut into the wall. It brimmed with darkness. The darkness whispered to us: come outside. I wondered if Mary heard it, too.

. . .

We found the logs in the morning. Half a cord, neatly stacked in the very place we'd been standing to watch the ship approach. All were two-foot long cylinders, three inches wide, with a lengthwise groove. We wondered if they weren't imitations, but after close inspection decided they really were wood.

Father stood with his hands on his hips and said, "Great. Just what we need." He gestured at the trees surrounding us. "More wood."

Mary and I laughed. Father eyed us, decided he'd made a good joke, and crinkled his eyes into a smile.

When the Overarching Event occurred, families like ours packed up and made for the hills like so many arks fleeing the waters. Mother and Father were confident they'd be able to sustain us. Priority had been given to seeds, staples, tools, and other necessities for life in the wild. It was a great adventure to Mary and me and we helped the family by imparting this to Lisa and Doug. We argued over who got to use which hoe and shovel, so eager were we to till this new life. Our cabin was a decrepit log structure that Mother and Father rebuilt, filling the chinks in the wood with plaster and adding the small sleeping room for us.

The outside world had been full of bellows and screeches and choking odors. We couldn't imagine a place for us in all that mess. How happy the prospect to build our own little life in the woods, on this ridge, was. Mother and Father assured us that if things got better, one day we might be able to return home—if we felt like it.

We doubted we'd ever want to.

How we delighted, when we first got here, at the earth responding to our tender care. How we prized our callouses. How we delighted in saving a portion of our harvest in jars for the winter. Our life in the lowlands was a dream, while the dirt and the woods here were real. Father went to the market for grains occasionally, a small smudge of shame that we were not entirely self-sufficient as some families were. But we had to feed the few animals we had so that they, in return, could feed us.

Three months ago, at the end of our second spring, we felt we'd succeeded. We'd met the challenge of the Overarching Event and prevailed.

We didn't know about soils at that time, and we didn't know about clouds. We didn't know that a change in both could result in hunger. We didn't know hunger.

For no reason we could decipher, as summer went on, our parents' magic failed. We got barely a handful of stunted fruit from the once-promiscuous zucchini plants. It was the altitude, they said. The cold nights, the short growing season, the fickleness of the gods, the strange new ripples.

Their frustration and bafflement at the withering garden and skinnying animals frightened us. Jenny the dog's rations were cut, and she whined at the dinner table. Father shooed her into a corner, and she whined from there. Her hunger made us feel guilty for having even a little to eat.

We'd been foraging all along, but we spent more time gathering roots, mushrooms, and berries from the wild. We added pine seeds, clover, thistle, pennycress, anything Mother said was safe to eat. We gnawed on small branches just to have something in our mouths, something to bite back at the gnawing in our stomachs.

Mother and Father talked about what had to be done for winter. Set more traps. Ration the staples, feed the animals what we could, and eat them when the feed was gone. Hope for an early spring.

"I can risk a bullet to fell a deer," Father said. "But if I miss—" The rifle and our handful of bullets were for emergencies only.

The phrase "if I miss" haunted us. We imagined a doe in his sights being hit, but not mortally. She staggers, wounded, deeper into the woods, where she bleeds out with no deer family to attend to her.

What if that happened to us? I had vague images of us setting out, when the day came, for help. But there was no help any more. We'd collapse on a mountainside, die in a blizzard, fall prey to wolves and marauders.

And then the logs. A final insult, even if Father had managed a joke.

"Well," said Mary, "at least we won't have to chop firewood for winter."

Father shook his head, the moment of humor gone. We knew what was going through his mind. Fate had set itself against him. It was just what you'd expect, *just* what you would expect, that in our hour of desperation, this thing from the sky would bring us the one thing we didn't need, like offering a drink of water to a drowning person.

. . .

It came again, and this time we were sure it was not a cloud. It could not have been because the clouds that day were low and gray, a little too intimate, smothering us in mist and rain, portions of which came dripping through the wooden slats and sheaves on the roof.

We were helping Mother and Father repair leaks in the rear of the house when Mary spotted something in the sky. She and I, followed by the little ones, went around front, into the clearing. The ship was gray, nearly indistinguishable from the clouds, but decorated with glowing lights. The rain did not douse them, which told us they were something other than flame. Phosphorescence, Mary suggested. That was our first clue that the ship was bringing a new science, one unknown to our remote little spot.

Lisa held Jenny the dog so she wouldn't bark. We watched the thing float there, like a stray puff of cloud, lowering slowly, lowering and lowering. We saw it was solid. Yes, a ship. We felt the hum in our stomachs and on the bottoms of our feet. Upon what tide it lowered we could not tell.

Oh, how we longed to know who captained it. But Father called out for us to bring him something, and Mother repeated the call, and like a herd stampeding in fright we ran around to the back of the cabin. Lisa forgot Jenny who, though she kept silent, was the only one who saw what happened next.

After we finished fixing the roof, I went around front. The ship was gone, but a new load of logs had been left. When Father saw them, he cursed and railed against the gods. Mother objected to his language.

"We've been doing it all wrong!" he shouted. "The gods have no loyalty. They're like cats, who never have to toil as humans do, and who need us only so they can be fed and adored. It's the Onegod who will take care of us!"

We'd heard this word before. He pronounced it Won-god. When I looked over his shoulder as he wrote his journal, he wrote it ONEGOD. It meant—well, he spent a great deal of time telling us what it meant. The notion had been bubbling and brewing in his brain. Soon we'd feel its full force.

Mother did not argue. I thought she would, but at the dinner table she let stand what Father said about matters above. She talked about cats instead. Their mysterious ways. Haunting looks, careful steps, flicking tails. We'd only seen pictures. They'd been eaten or had fled to some refuge after the Overarching Event.

Father refused to burn the logs. We thought the energy we saved from chopping could be put into foraging, but if we made excuses not to cut wood, his shoulders sagged and conveyed disgust at him having to do all the work.

Mary was the one, after a few days, who carried logs in for the fire. Father knew but didn't say anything, and the woodcutting work tapered off. The first inch of autumn snow fell and we began our preparations for the months when everything would be buried under three feet of it. We repaired the snowshoes, filled the chinks in the cabin walls with new plaster, and shored up sagging timbers.

Then food began to appear. Mary and Lisa usually were the ones to find it: squash on the dying vines, berries on the bushes, a sudden proliferation of mushrooms in the woods—inexplicable so late in the season. The goat gave more milk than before, the chickens more eggs, and the baleful look in their eyes melted away like the first snow.

"Onegod," Father said. "It's because we've been praying."

We hadn't, but he had. We still whispered our prayers in the old way and we still treasured the nights when Mother told us one of her tales. She said they were just old stories, but Mary and I were sharp enough to pick out which "fairies" resembled which gods. We were convinced she secretly sang the old songs, too, softly under her breath, while she was working in the kitchen or carrying water from the spring.

We gathered the marvelous food, filling our stomachs at night and storing the rest away for winter. Little speculation was made about its genesis. No one wanted to scare away our luck.

Father looked over the miraculously fructifying

garden with unwarranted pride. He scratched Jenny behind the ears and told her she needed go on no more excursions.

Jenny had taken, in the starving summer months, to running away. I listened for her to be scratching at the door all through the first night, and she didn't. I went out to sit with the moon. Wolves howled, and I shivered thinking of Jenny out there.

Two nights she was gone. Father declared the bears or wolves had gotten her. We were desolate. I heard the wolves again the second night and wondered if they were howling over her carcass.

Yet there she was at our doorstep the next morning. Blood covered her snout. Battles with predators, we assumed, though she had only a few scratches on the rest of her body. Her coat didn't press into her ribs as it had before. We let her inside and she sniffed everything as if it might be food.

The next time she disappeared, we didn't worry as much. When the wolves set to howling, I wondered if her voice might be among them. She returned again, but seemed distant, as if we were no longer her pack. She looked at Lisa and Doug in an appraising way. She'd learned something out there from whatever world she visited.

What a relief it was when the logs solved all of that. Jenny the dog now slept contentedly by the fire and at our feet. The prospect of winter no longer chilled us.

■　■　■

Moonlight makes a strange sound. The sound is no

sound, yet it amplifies the silence. Silence, as our parents taught us when we first arrived here in the woods, was only the absence of a screen that had blocked out the inner roar: the sound of the blood coursing through your veins and air bellowing through your lungs. The only true silence—they did not hesitate to say, since we'd already seen plenty of it—was death.

I'd go outside some nights because I couldn't sleep. I couldn't sleep because I heard a call. I can't say if it came from within or without. In stillness all things begin.

I went out, wool blanket draped over my shoulders, to listen. Listening confirmed my existence. If wolves weren't howling nor owls hooting nor wind whipping, I heard the inner roar and could be still.

Inside, in my sleeping bag, the walls wakened me with the clamor from outside. They were all around us. I didn't know who "they" were, but I was determined to find out. I wriggled out of the bag while my siblings slept and snorted. I padded to the door and slid the bolt bit by bit, so its scrape could be heard only by a nearby spider. I went out and sat on a stump, huddled in my blanket. The deep forest night, caressed by moonlight, enfolded my brain. Where had "they" gone?

Over the many nights, an accumulation of hours and darkness and moonlight of various shades, I became acquainted with them. They were all around. Trees, straight and tall or tortured and bent, barely daring to whisper. Huffs from the earth. Critters skittering. Creaks from the logs of the cabin. The unheard scream of the stars. All of it extending out to the ridges near and far and farther, beyond what my eye conjectured.

Some of us are strange. We're not sure we belong here. A part of us seems left behind, in another world. Not the one from which we'd fled, but the one before that. Strangeness needs companionship, and I am blessed to have come from the same kernel as my sister Mary.

That's why it took me some time to absorb what I found one November night, a few weeks after a second set of logs had been deposited by the ship of clouds.

The moon was high and bright. It came crashing in through the window. I didn't think to look at the others as I slipped out of my sleeping bag. It had snowed that afternoon, a couple of inches. The engorged moon and the snow combined to light the landscape uncannily, as if the days of electricity had come back, and a party was being thrown, and no one came. Just me, out there squinting at shadows that seemed scissored out of the white paper of snowy ground.

The stillness was too bright on nights like this, the brightness too loud. The top layer of snow had been crusted by cold and made a toast-like crunch with every step. I sat on my stump and gazed at my battered boots and the trail they'd made—and that was when I saw the other trail. Shoe shapes in the snow made by feet similar in size to mine, the rims edged by shadow, fresher than if they'd been made in daytime, as if I or my double had been out here once already tonight.

I stood and followed them past the shed for the animals, which was quiet, into the trees and around to the top of a small ledge. The six-foot rock wall had been an exciting discovery when we first arrived, something we could scale up and slide down through cracks in the ledge where grasses grew. It was, in our imaginations, a fort from which we'd repel invaders. A small recess in the rock, which we called a cave, gave us a place to hide.

A ghostly-faint orange-yellow light danced on the snow below me. I wasn't afraid, given the size of the footprints and my familiarity with the ledge, until I saw the light. I slid down the snow in one of the cracks and crept around to where I could see the recess.

The light came from a candle anchored in the ground, the flame lightly licking the walls of the cave, casting a warm glimmer on the face of the girl who sat cross-legged inside, cradling one of the logs the ship had left. She hummed to it in a soft voice. I was startled by the scene. Why would Mary be out in the dead of night bestowing such tender care on a length of wood?

She didn't look up until I approached. "Hi, Jake." She'd figured out, from the sliding and crunching, that someone was coming.

"How'd you know it was me?"

"Had to be."

More logs were stacked around her in the cave. I crouched. "What are you doing?"

"Taking care of them." She looked into my eyes. "You know what they mean for us."

"Of course. The food came after they came."

She shifted. The candle flame bent, breathed a puff of smoke, and straightened. She held the log out to me. "Tuck your bare fingers into the groove."

I got on my knees to take it. The way she offered it in two arms reminded me of when Lisa and Doug had arrived. Tiny, delicate mummies. Gifts from the sky, Father said, and the earth. How Mother held them, how she taught us to hold them. How impossibly small their faces were, until they exploded into a red squall. How the mummies grew into clumsy little creatures who got into everything, then into smaller versions of us, requiring patience and explanations. It was that early reverence that came back to me now in the way Mary handled the logs. I wondered if she was losing her mind.

Which would mean I was losing her.

I shook off a mitten and did as Mary said. I tucked in four fingers. My mouth dropped, my eyes widened.

"You felt the tingle?"

I nodded. A little buzz, as if electricity still existed. I kept my fingers there. The log warmed them.

"More food will come tomorrow," Mary said. "I'm glad you know now."

Her eyes were in mine. Her voice was the one we used when we really meant it. "You could have—" I stopped myself. "We can't tell Father. Even if he believes it, who knows what he'd do."

"Which also means we can't tell Mother."

I nodded. She'd feel obliged to share a secret this big. "That's why you hide the logs out here."

"We can't burn them anymore." Father had taken

to using an occasional log in the wood stove. "We don't know if more will come."

"Okay," I said.

"It's our secret."

It was, but I didn't answer her. It hurt that it wasn't our secret until now. Before that, it had been her secret.

I handed the log back to her and stood up. "Do you want to go in?"

She set the log among the others with her special care, blew out the candle, and followed me through the moonlight that pressed down so harshly upon us that night.

.   .   .

Mary fell asleep quickly. But the moon was still out there, and I lay awake in my bag, questions jumping through my brain. Why hadn't Mary told me how to care for the logs as soon as she figured it out? Why'd she hide them without telling me? We shared everything—triumphs and defeats, secrets and fantasies, likes and dislikes. Until now.

A mouse was scraping at something behind a wall. It taunted my fears. Skritch, skritch. Mary was growing apart from me. Skritch, skritch. The logs spoke to her in a private humming language. Skritch, skritch. They wanted to divide us. Skritch, skritch, skritch. Mary had taken possession of the logs—or vice-versa. They belonged to each other now.

Another part of my mind answered: If that's so, why'd she reveal her secret when I found her?

Why'd she let me tuck my fingers in? Why was I permitted to hide the logs, too? We'd have to find places beside the cave, which was getting full—I'd have to talk to her about that in the morning—.

I made it my duty, from then on, to chop wood from the forest. I turned myself into a regular woodcutter's son. It gave me something to do during the fallow November days. It was also a channel for my fears about Mary. Each chunk I cracked, split, and stacked was a worry dispatched.

The woodcutting pleased Father inordinately. He took it as a signal of our gratitude and obeisance. It inspired him to speak more about Onegod at dinner. The big difference between Onegod and the others was that Onegod cares what humans do, favors and watches over us, while the others are like cats who'd eat their humans if ever they stopped being fed by them. Onegod wants only our devotion. I wondered if that didn't make him more greedy than the gods who desired mere offerings, but I dared not voice the question.

Mary acted no different, at least not to the eye. A serenity floated like a mist of invisible attendants around her, though that could have come as easily from our full stomachs and knowledge of the source of the bounty as from her secret. Mother seemed no different, and Father was changed only in his enthusiasm for Onegod.

One night, as she was putting us to bed, I asked Mother for a tale. They'd been a source of comfort during the lean days. I asked shyly, fearing Onegod might have forbidden the telling of tales.

Mother gave me that smile of understanding she

gives when she sees we're troubled in a way we can't say. She waited until we were all in our bags with clean teeth and faces, then sat cross-legged in the threshold, as if to block out demons and create a special space.

I was hoping her understanding extended so far as to realize I wanted a tale that fit with my new role in the world. Instead, she chose one we'd heard before. My heart clutched at her choice and made me wonder if I understood her understanding at all.

It was the one about the ogre who takes in a child who's wandered from home and into the woods. The first time we heard it, the child was named Jake. This time she was named Mary.

The ogre is kind to Mary. He feeds her delicious food from his farm and all she has to do is clear the table, wash the dishes, and sweep the floor. She gets plump and bored, though, and asks to return home. The ogre is sad, but gives her a parting gift, a magic donkey to ride. The magic is that if you say "hoogleboogle" to it, gold will drop out of its behind like poop.

Doug and Lisa giggled when poop was mentioned. Mother gave them a look of mock admonishment.

Mary thanked the ogre and went on her way. Halfway home, she stopped at an inn for the night. She said the magic word to the donkey and out came the gold, which she used to pay for her room. The innkeeper saw this, and while Mary slept substituted a different donkey in the stable for hers. Mary arrived home to shouting and surprise and tears of joy but also scolding. She said not to worry; she had something that would allow them to live in plenty for the rest of their lives. She brought in the donkey and said, "Hoogleboogle!"

Nothing happened. Mary shouted the word at him again and again and at last, the donkey produced. But it wasn't gold, just regular poop. Mary's father chased her out of the house.

Back into the woods she went, back to the inn to get what was hers. The innkeeper used a big club to drive her away. The ogre's house was her only refuge.

The ogre chuckled at her mistake with the innkeeper but took her back. Again, after a period of bounty, Mary missed her family and told the ogre she wanted to go home. Though sad, he gave her a new gift. It was an ordinary-looking tablecloth, except that if you opened it while saying "moobywooby," it produced jewels, candlesticks, and fine silverware.

Mary had to stop at the inn again because it was the only one between the ogre's house and her home. The innkeeper saw the tablecloth and recommended she give it to him for safekeeping. Mary made the mistake of warning him not to open it and for sure never to say "moobywooby."

The innkeeper grinned and nodded and, of course, did exactly that and, when he saw the riches, swapped Mary's tablecloth for a different one. Mary arrived home to great hoopla again, followed by even more rebuke when the tablecloth produced the same results as the donkey, minus the poop.

For a third time Mary found herself back at the farm of the ogre, who had another laugh at her expense. She told herself that it was interesting, after all, to live with an ogre, so long as he was a nice one.

The inevitable day came when she was ready to leave. The ogre gave her a carved wooden walking stick. He warned her never to speak the word "bongletongle" in its presence. Mary, always curious, tried it out on the road. The stick leaped out of her hand and beat her about the head and shoulders until she crumpled in a heap.

At the inn, she warned the salivating innkeeper about "bongletongle." Naturally he stole the stick from her room as she slept. She wakened to the sounds of the stick smacking the innkeeper and his wife in every part of their bodies, then smacking pans and shelves and dishes and glasses and vases and anything that could be smashed or splintered. No one got much sleep that night.

In the morning, Mary found the stick waiting outside her door. She picked it up and, singing a little song to herself, headed home on her original donkey, which she'd found in the stable. What a surprise her parents were in for.

We laughed and clapped, and Mother kissed us goodnight.

We murmured bongletongle to one another until we fell asleep. In my dreams, I heard the logs bongletongling in the night.

How different the story seemed from the first time Mother had told it. This time, I took it to mean that Mother knew what Mary had discovered. Maybe she knew we were hiding the logs in the woods. An adventure in the woods had given the Mary in the story new powers. Maybe Mother was recognizing we had new powers, too.

I closed my eyes to this pleasant thought. But the mouse was awake and began its skritch, skritch, skritch. Was it all of us who had the new powers, or just Mary? And if that was the case, where was the place for me, aside from chopping wood?

.   .   .

Over the next many nights, I woke in the still hours, as usual. The first thing I did was to check if Mary was in her sleeping bag. She was, every time. Some nights I went out to sit on my stump. Some I didn't and just lay there wondering what she was dreaming.

Winter came. Long dark nights bent over our books under a candle or oil lamp. Mary and I talked about what we read as if nothing was wrong. She gave me a look, when I made a remark about the "magic logs," that let me know she felt I was acting strange. Maybe it was just the inevitability of growing apart by growing up.

New kinds of food appeared. Apples, miraculously red in the snow. Grass and seed for the animals, suddenly in the shed. Fish, frozen near the woodpile. Father never asked how fish could get up to our ridge. We reached an unspoken understanding with him. He knew we believed the logs were the source of our plenitude, and though he'd never say it aloud, he accepted it.

We claimed no victory. We wanted to avoid bongletongle at all costs.

I went in search of ever more wood to chop.

Warmth was urgent, with the logs now safe from the maw of the iron stove. I served a purpose after all.

One morning Mary said, "Let's get our snowshoes."

I did, automatically, but as we strapped on the leather thongs, I said, "What for?"

She went to the end of the long pile of wood, protected by a roof of rough slats, where the remaining logs were stacked. We'd been taking them, a few at a time, to our caches in the woods.

"We don't need to do this anymore," I said.

"You never know."

Arms weighed with logs, the snowshoes making us walk like ducks, we went into the woods. Mother caught a glimpse of us from the kitchen window and turned away, hiding her smile. We deposited the logs in a snow cave we'd dug on the opposite side of the cabin from the ledge.

Mary stood breathing hard after dropping the logs, clouds of steam obscuring her face from mine in the cold air.

"Are you afraid the others will steal them?"

She bent, hands to knees, then let herself fall backward into the soft snow. I tilted back, too. The snow was deep enough to provide each of us with a kind of easy chair.

"That's a weird question," she said.

"No one's burning them. Why hide them?"

"To keep them safe."

"Or to make up for the fact you were the first one to burn them?"

She blew out a long breath, admiring the stream of mist from within. "I think we should tell Lisa and

Doug how they work. Don't you?"

"I guess. Father doesn't want to hear about it. Mother may know, but doesn't want to say."

"What if something happens to us?" Quickly Mary waved her mittened hands. "I don't think it will, but—the others need to know. Just in case."

"Yes." This was making me feel better.

"And one day, we might—"

I waited and waited, and finally said, "Die?"

"No! No, we might go away. You know, when we get older and we want to, you know—go out into the world."

"Together?"

Her eyebrows jumped. "Of course!"

My heart jumped. I thought of all the nights since November that I'd woken and checked if Mary was there in the room. Always she was. I wondered why, if she'd been out that one night, she didn't go out again. It came to me that the only reason she went out was that she knew I went out, sometimes, to sit and listen to the stars. Now she didn't need to anymore.

I was full of questions. All of them started: Why? The old skritchy ones fell away, and I asked the one I'd been so desperate to ever since the wood had arrived.

"What *are* the logs? Where did they come from?"

"I keep wondering." She leaned forward, eager to talk. "From the gods?"

"There aren't stories of the gods flying in ships. Or delivering wood. Father thinks it's Onegod, but—logs?"

Mary giggled at how absurd the whole thing

seemed. "What if they're produced by some kind of knowledge elsewhere? A long way out there."

Suddenly we were back to normal with each other. How strange these things are. What's nearest is sometimes what's most mysterious.

We discussed our ideas about the origin of the logs. Father was sure it was not terrestrial, and we agreed. It was extraterrestrial, beyond our little patch of earth. Some kind of science we'd never conceived. Remarkable knowledge courtesy of a faraway place, bestowed upon us across the sea of sky by ships of cloud. Maybe they were flying overhead and heard Jenny's howls when she was on foray. Maybe Jenny knew more than she could tell us. Maybe one day we'd learn the language of the hum in our stomachs.

This became our new faith. We'd been sharing it, though today was the first time we shared the words. But we knew what each other meant, and we hoped the ship would return so that we could interrogate its coordinates. Who are you? What are you? Why are you helping us?

And, until we were given a chance to ask, the biggest question of all: How do we gauge our knowledge of how much we don't yet know?

. . .

Father indulged our superstition. That's what he called it. We mutually understood that we each had our own ways of understanding the workings of fortune.

The one thing we all knew, and all shared, was

the garden. Spring came along and we dug into it with relish. No matter what the logs might provide, we yearned to till after the lassitude of winter.

Doug was, as always, the one to say the obvious. He was young enough never to be bored. "I don't really need to do this, do I?"

He was rewarded with a lesson from Father. "My son, you cannot get something for nothing. Provender comes from our dedication and devotion. Hard work has been and always will be our salvation. We cannot know Onegod's ways."

I wanted to burst out, "But we saw the ship! We felt the hum!"

I did not burst out. We all were stuck here together, for the time being. Working the garden was not so bad. Foraging offered a chance to go into the woods. Who knew what else we'd discover there?

Mary and I talked, when we had the chance, about the far place from which the ships came. Sometimes we let Lisa and Doug listen. Jenny cocked an ear. Maybe it was from the other side of the world. Maybe the sky is a sea with cloud-island civilizations of its own and they communicate in hums we barely perceive. Maybe the Moon is an island. Mother said it was inhabited by rail-like beings who rippled in the wind and changed size and shape, like smoke from a campfire. So different from us that we could not comprehend their ways.

We did not know. That was the thing that got us.

We did not know.

We did not know.

We did not know.

Yet Father thought he did. It was maddening. He imposed this verdict upon us: He knew. We didn't.

We knew we didn't, but could he really know that he did, really? Did he ever ask himself how he knew what he knew, and how he knew how much he didn't know? Can he know that we will not discover unknown waveforms that someday give us the means to sail into the sky and float among the clouds, to go bounding among the stars and greet travelers in the great flow of traffic up there—there in what appears to us now to be empty, silent space?

The skies are vast. The seas are vast. Our beliefs come to us, they are handed down like brown or blue or green eyes. We have no instrument by which to measure their truth. It's as if Father declared: We all must have blue eyes now, because Onegod has blue eyes and we are made in His image.

Mother has told me, and my siblings tell me, that I do not have blue eyes. Yet Father expects me to believe I do. Am I supposed to dye them blue, make them pretty?

He is Father, and I will not disobey him so long as he lives. Nor will I defy him, not openly. He and Mother saved us from the Overarching Event, and brought us here, and cared for us. But quietly, in hidden recesses of our minds, Mary and I nurture our thoughts. The same way that, through unspoken labyrinths, like flows of water under the earth, Mother imparts her knowledge through her tales. Occasionally, when she thinks no one is looking, she picks up a log and caresses it the way she's seen us do.

. . .

Father has become mystical now, a few years on, lacing his lectures on gardening with spiritual insights and memories from childhood, a subject he's never spoken about before. Out of nowhere, he'll say, "Time, the real sandman, buries us all. Never forget that."

There are still inevitabilities, is what I think he's reminding us.

Father tills the soil, though it causes his knees no end of pain. Mother does too, and we, with Lisa and Doug, help as much as we can. Mary and I have reached the age when you think about setting out from the family bosom. We talk of journeys to nearby hills to reconnoiter and see what has become of the other families and to learn what the Overarching Event has wrought. Maybe we'll see the ship again, the ship for which we have craned and pained our necks so many times. We watch Jenny every day for a sign. We listen. We listen very hard.

Most of all, we think about meeting with others, which will enable us, at the right time, to start our own families: happy visions of young cousins cavorting—in a respectful way—with our portion of the logs.

Father still doesn't trust them. He's afraid they'll suddenly turn mephitic or betray us to an enemy. We have to remember the principles of farming, Father warns, and remember Onegod, because there will come a day when we need them both.

We still don't know what we don't know. We're stuck, yet moving forward, as all animals do.

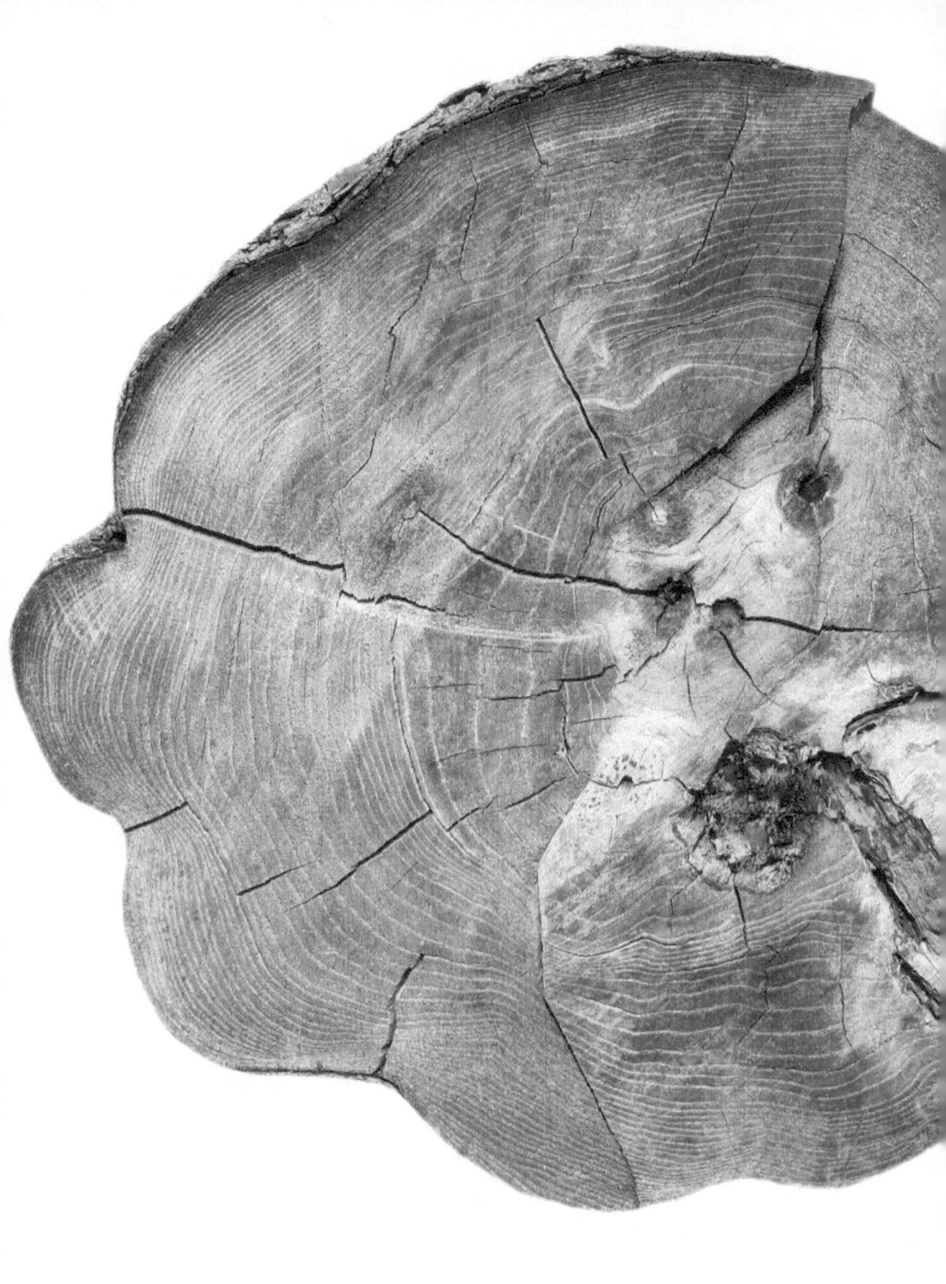

[contributor bios]

Rebekah Bergman's fiction has been published or is forthcoming in *Hobart, Joyland, Passages North, Poor Claudia, Two Serious Ladies,* and *The Nashville Review,* among other journals. She holds an MFA from The New School and is a contributing editor of *NOON.*

Kevin Finucane was awarded a bronze Solas Award by *Travelers' Tales* in creative nonfiction in 2009 and was named a Finalist for the Faulkner-Wisdom Competition in the novella category for 2010.

Matthew Kirkpatrick is the author of *Diary of a Pennsylvania Farmer* (Throwback Books, forthcoming), *The Exiles* (Ricochet Editions), and *Light Without Heat* (FC2). His fiction and essays have appeared in *The Rumpus, The Common, Puerto del Sol, Denver Quarterly, Believer Logger, Notre Dame Review,* and elsewhere. His audio collage and hypertext, "The Silent Numbers" is anthologized in the *Electronic Literature Collection, Volume 3,* and was part of the "Shapeshifting Texts" exhibit at the University of Bremen. He is an assistant professor at Eastern Michigan University where he teaches fiction and new media writing.

[contributor bios]

Rachel Lyon's debut novel *Self-Portrait with Boy* is forthcoming from Scribner in February 2018. Her short work has appeared in *Joyland, Iowa Review, McSweeney's,* and other publications. Rachel teaches for Sackett Street Writers Workshop, Catapult, and elsewhere and is a cofounder of the reading series Ditmas Lit in her native Brooklyn. Visit her at www.rachellyon.work.

J. L. Montavon was born and raised in Denver and lives in San Francisco. The story "Recursions" was chosen by Joan Wickersham as the winner of the 2016 Salamander Fiction Prize. Other stories have appeared in *Hobart* and *Prime Number Magazine.*

Simone Person grew up in small Michigan towns and Toledo, Ohio. She is a dual MFA/MA in Fiction and African American and African Diaspora Studies at Indiana University. Her work has appeared in *Queen Mob's Teahouse* and *Puerto del Sol,* among others, and has been anthologized in *Crab Fat Magazine: Best of Year Three.* Her chapbook is a semifinalist selection for *Honeysuckle Press*'s 2017 Chapbook Contest. She occasionally uses Twitter and Instagram at @princxporkchop.

[contributor bios]

Jay Vera Summer is a Chicagoan living in Florida. She writes fiction and creative nonfiction, and co-founded *weirderary*, an online literary magazine, and First Draft, a monthly live literary event in Tampa. Her writing has been published in marieclaire. com, *Proximity*, *LimeHawk*, *theEEEL*, and *Chicago Literati*.

Tamara K. Walker resides in Colorado and writes short fiction and poetry, often of a surreal, irreal, magical realist, experimental, speculative or otherwise unusual nature. Her fiction has previously appeared in *The Cafe Irreal*, *A cappella Zoo*, *Melusine*, *Peculiar Mormyrid*, *ink&coda*, *Three Minute Plastic*, and others. Her poetry has appeared or is forthcoming in *Star*Line*, *Lavender Review*, *Scifaikuest*, and *indefinite space*, among others. Her short story, "Camisole", which appeared in *The Conium Review: Vol. 4*, was a 2015 Pushcart Prize nominee. She may be found online at http://tamarakwalker.weebly.com.

Stephanie Wang is a Beijing-born Australian writer currently living in Melbourne. She can travel in time, but only in one direction. She is currently working on a novel.